SO-BTE-893

"You're A Disby-Looking Female, All Right.

"But I'm not so hard up that I'd take what you've got to offer." Travis started to brush past her.

"It's not on offer to you, at any rate," Joanna snapped. "I'll wait till I get back to civilization, thank you."

Travis reached down and captured her wrist, pulling it upward between them. Her fingers were balled into a tight knot. "This fist shows you're not so civilized yourself, *lady!*" he said scornfully. "But you're smart not to try and use it."

Joanna just managed to flick her fingers against his cheek. "Oh, no?" she mocked.

Fire flashed in his gray eyes. "A challenge, is it?" he rasped before his head came down and his hard mouth covered hers.

BARBARA TURNER

used to devote her literary endeavors to seeing stage plays and writing them. Then she discovered the delights of contemporary romances, and now she finds that writing romantic novels takes up most of her creative time. Married, with no children, she says, "My pleasures are bound up in an abiding interest in the world around me; in the people I meet, in their fascinating idiosyncrasies, and in the new places and exciting experiences I find because I go looking for them."

Dear Reader:

I'd like to take this opportunity to thank you for all your support and encouragement of Silhouette Romances.

Many of you write in regularly, telling us what you like best about Silhouette, which authors are your favorites. This is a tremendous help to us as we strive to publish the best contemporary romances possible.

All the romances from Silhouette Books are for you, so enjoy this book and the many stories to come.

Karen Solem
Editor-in-Chief
Silhouette Books

BARBARA TURNER
Cassie Come Home

Silhouette Romance

Published by Silhouette Books New York

America's Publisher of Contemporary Romance

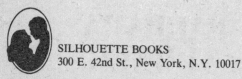

SILHOUETTE BOOKS
300 E. 42nd St., New York, N.Y. 10017

Copyright © 1985 by Barbara Turner

Distributed by Pocket Books

All rights reserved, including the right to reproduce
this book or portions thereof in any form whatsoever.
For information address Silhouette Books,
300 E. 42nd St., New York, N.Y. 10017

ISBN: 0-373-08350-5

First Silhouette Books printing March, 1985

10 9 8 7 6 5 4 3 2 1

All of the characters in this book are fictitious. Any resem-
blance to actual persons, living or dead, is purely coincidental.

Map by Ray Lundgren

Silhouette, Silhouette Romance and
colophon are registered trademarks of the publisher.

America's Publisher of Contemporary Romance

Printed in the U.S.A.

To Miranda Coffey and Neff Rotter,
for their invaluable aid and encouragement
in helping Cassie come home

Cassie Come Home

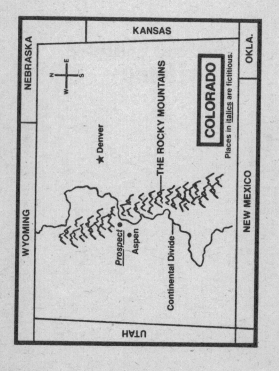

Chapter One

Could there be anything more bleak, Joanna wondered, than a small town bus terminal at night? Her eyes traveled from the fly-specked face of the large clock above the ticket counter to the cracked and peeling paint on the walls. A faded poster depicting the glories of the Rocky Mountains was thumbtacked alongside a chalkboard listing the weekly bus schedule to and from Prospect, Colorado. Not exactly the place she would have chosen to get stranded in, but that was the problem. She didn't have any choice.

Tired of sitting so long, Joanna rose from her seat in the shabby row of hard chairs near the side window. She stretched briefly, easing stiff muscles. The venetian blind that should have covered the window was broken, and the cold fluorescent light from the fixture overhead spilled onto the street outside, making a stark oasis of light in the backstreet neighborhood. She peered out to see if there was any letup in the downpour of rain that had followed a spectacular display of summer thunder and lightning shortly after she had gotten off the bus an hour before.

The rain seemed to be slackening. At least it served to make her grateful for the shelter the deserted waiting room provided. Turning from the window with a small sigh, she sat down again and tried to relax.

"Looks like whoever's gonna pick you up got held up in the storm, don't it?"

Joanna gave an involuntary start as the night clerk spoke to her from the ticket window. She gave him a noncommittal shrug, hoping it would put him off, but he settled his elbows on the counter for a chat. He reminded her of an inquisitive mouse as his beaky nose twitched and his small dark eyes ran over her yet again, seeking a clue to her prolonged presence in his terminal so late at night.

She didn't think he'd get much satisfaction. Her drab raincoat had no style; she'd seen it on hundreds of other women, and its bulky folds gave no clues about her shape or size. The scarf tied peasant style under her chin made her face look almost, if not quite, plain. The medium-sized suitcase on the floor beside her chair was ordinary, well-used; it would tell no secrets.

"Not many folks get off the Denver bus on the late run through Prospect." The nasal voice paused, then prodded hopefully: "Visiting kin, are you? There's a phone you can use, if you want to give them a call."

"No, thanks, I think I'll just wait." Joanna's voice was husky from her long silence. It didn't quite match the colorlessness of her appearance.

The clerk tried again. "I know most of the folks hereabouts. Nobody mentioned they was expecting anyone tonight."

Joanna settled down into her seat and closed her eyes, ignoring the conversational overture. The clerk snorted and retired once more to the parcel room in the rear.

She was relieved he'd given up. She needed to think. Her fingers tightened on the purse she held in her lap as she considered its meager contents. Two dollars and seventeen cents wouldn't even buy a decent meal, let alone a place to sleep.

But then, she hadn't had much time to think about finances in the flurry of making her escape from the hotel and the city. She was fortunate she'd had enough cash to get her this far.

Too bad she'd had to leave Denver. The mile-high city, pulsing with an exciting mixture of boomtown roughness and sophisticated urban culture, had fascinated and entertained her ever since she had arrived there six months ago. But it was no place for her now. Gerald would hunt for her there, first.

She could expect him to put a couple of his strong-arm boys on her trail when he found she hadn't taken refuge with any of her friends in Denver. Gerald had enough reason to hunt her down. Those oil-lease options she had taken from his briefcase were worth a fortune, not to mention the blow she'd given his male vanity. He'd been so sure she was finally going to give in to his efforts to get her into his bed.

The thought of encountering her ex-boss in his present state of mind made her shiver. During the months she had worked as his secretary at Lasker Development Corporation, she'd seen ample evidence of Gerald Lasker's temper; he was vengeful when it was aroused. Ruthless, willing to operate on the outer fringes of the law when it suited him, Gerald wouldn't be bothered by scruples where she was concerned. Certainly he wouldn't be impressed by her motives, either for turning him down, or for interfering in his affairs. Joanna hoped she'd covered her tracks well enough to give her time to get out of his reach.

She breathed a silent prayer that the clerk at the busy Denver terminal who had sold her the bus ticket wouldn't remember her. With the help of the borrowed raincoat and scarf, no makeup, and keeping her eyes lowered, she had deliberately made herself forgettable. She hoped.

Joanna stretched her long slender legs into a more comfortable position. The aroma of fresh-perking coffee coming from the parcel room in the back reached her, and her nostrils flared in appreciation. She resisted the temptation to go to the ticket window and ask the clerk if he could spare a cup of his coffee. The inevitable conversation that would follow would be more than she could handle; she was bone tired and her nerves had suffered enough during the hectic events of the last twelve hours. She felt she had aged a decade beyond her twenty-five years.

She considered the possibilities open to her. If she waited here in the bus station until daylight, she could try to hitch a ride through the mountains, maybe get as far as Cheyenne. Work at some kind of low-profile job, perhaps? She'd worked as a waitress before, and at least she'd be able to eat while she built up some cash reserves.

If only she hadn't let her bank balance get so low this last month. It was too bad she hadn't been able to contact Donovan before she left the city. The old wildcatter would have loaned her enough to get by on for a while, and she would have been rid of the papers as well. Her foot eased alongside the suitcase, touching it as though it were loaded with a volatile explosive.

With a mental shrug of acceptance, Joanna rested her head as well as she could against the hard seat and settled herself to try to get some sleep. She didn't see the bright flash of headlights that shone through the windows of the terminal when a vehicle pulled up in the street outside. It was the sound of the door opening and a swift rush of cold, wet air that brought her head up. Her eyes widened and a rush of adrenaline turned her mouth acid. My God, she thought, her brain still clouded with half-dreams of pursuers and vengeance. They've found me already!

The man who stood in the doorway had thick dark hair that glistened with raindrops as he turned his head to scan the room. His eyes settled on Joanna. The harsh glare of the fluorescent light drained his face of color and expression, and Joanna braced herself as the man moved toward her in a few space-eating strides. She found the strength to rise to her feet to meet him, her face taut, paler than his, though in her case it was not only the fault of the lighting. The man came to a halt in front of her.

"So you did come," he said abrasively, his voice deep. His eyes were bleakly gray.

Joanna stared back at him wordlessly, registering the height, the breadth of shoulder, the narrow-boned face set in hard lines. He looked about as friendly as an axe. She responded with a defensive hardening of her own features; her hands knotted into fists.

"You . . ." Her voice caught in her throat and failed her. Before she could clear it, he spoke again.

"I'm Travis Carlyle." The dark brows maintained their uncompromising straight line. "I've come to take you out to the ranch."

For a moment Joanna thought she hadn't heard him right. What was he talking about? Gerald had nothing to do with any ranch; his business was oil. "The . . . ranch," she repeated slowly, playing for time. He reached for her suitcase.

"No!" She protested sharply. She moved to stop him, and their hands touched. They both pulled back abruptly from the contact.

He stared at her, his eyebrows elevating. "What is it? You sent the telegram, lady. ARRIVING 9 P.M. BY BUS FROM DENVER. And here you are."

Automatically Joanna glanced at the big clock. Its hands stood at half past ten. She looked back at the tall stranger and found that the shock of his sudden appearance was wearing off. This time she took in the well-worn ranch clothes he was wearing. Boots, blue jeans, and a checked shirt; a sheepskin jacket that had seen years of all-weather service. The clothes obviously were the real thing, not the pseudocowboy outfit sometimes affected by city-dwelling macho types. This man was not pseudo anything. Besides, there hadn't been enough time. He couldn't possibly be one of Gerald's men, sent to find her and drag her back to Denver. He was just a stranger who had mistaken her for someone else.

Apparently the rancher or whatever he was took her lack of response as an accusation. "So I'm late," he said. "We didn't get your telegram until this afternoon, and I had a mare in trouble with a foal. Consider yourself lucky I'm here at all. Personally I'd just as soon you'd stayed in Denver." Antagonism radiated from him. "Are you coming out to the ranch or not?" he asked when she didn't react.

"How far is it?" Joanna didn't know what possessed her to ask the delaying question.

"Far enough. Sure you hadn't better stick around here and pick up the next bus back to the city?" A callused thumb gestured toward the chalkboard posted beside the ticket window. The next departure listed for Denver was noon the following day.

Joanna stared at the chart, her mind working rapidly. Obviously Travis Carlyle didn't know the woman he was supposed to meet. Just that he was to pick her up off the bus from Denver and take her to a ranch. "We," he'd said. Someone at the ranch would know he'd made a mistake as soon as she showed up there, if she were foolish enough to do what she was thinking of doing. Should she take the chance or not?

Out of the corner of her eye Joanna saw that the night clerk had returned to the ticket window and was listening with interest. She made a snap decision.

"I'll come with you, Mr. . . . Mr. Carlyle."

From the frown that darkened the rancher's brow, it was evident he was disappointed she wasn't going to take his suggestion to go back to Denver. Joanna couldn't help it; her lips curved in a small grin of commiseration.

He didn't like it. His narrow face became even more uncompromisingly set. Without further comment, he picked up her suitcase, nodded at the gawking night clerk, then strode toward the door. Drawing a deep breath, Joanna followed him.

It took a moment for her eyes to adjust to the darkness outside. The rain had diminished to no more than a few scattering drops. Stepping gingerly to avoid puddles, Joanna made her way toward the solidly built pickup truck parked in front of the building. Before she had time for second thoughts, he had stored the suitcase in a compartment behind the seat and helped her into the high cab. He took his place behind the steering wheel. With his hand on the ignition, he hesitated, then reached into the compartment again to pull out a woolly rug. He dropped it on her lap.

"Better wrap this around your legs. Gets drafty in here, even with the heater on," he said tersely.

His action surprised her, considering the sour attitude he'd shown her so far. She tucked the rug around her legs gratefully. Though it was still summer, the nighttime chill was a reminder that snow lingered on the high peaks year-round at these altitudes.

In a short time they passed through the city limits. Lulled by the deep-throated hum of the big motor, the darkness outside, and the silence of the man beside her, Joanna felt her tense muscles start to relax.

I'm taking a gamble, she admitted to herself, but it might work out just right. If Gerald's men came through Prospect asking about her, the night clerk could tell them that the only traveler that night had been expected and was accounted for. Country people were known for their hospitality to strangers, weren't they? She'd tell whoever was at the ranch that a mistake had been made; maybe she could work out some way of getting a lift to Cheyenne. Stifling a sigh, she knew the plan was weak, but it was the best she could do. At least she could hope to buy some breathing space, make it harder for Gerald's men to find her.

She glanced at the man beside her. Even in the near-darkness she could sense the coldness of his attitude toward her. Who would be waiting for them at the ranch? His wife, maybe. A man with the dark good looks this man had was bound to be married. If she wasn't the jealous type, his wife might be willing to help another woman in difficulties. She'd better hope she didn't have to tell her story to the hostile Travis.

They left the smooth surface of the highway and turned onto a road leading up through a canyon. Without the light from the moon, hidden overhead, the road was a black lonely tunnel winding endlessly upward. Her throat dry, Joanna swallowed, making an effort to hang on to her positive outlook.

"Arne called you Cassie. Short for Cassandra, right?" His voice was harsh, breaking the silence that had become increasingly heavy.

She'd have to answer. It was too soon to start with explanations. "Yes," she replied at last. What else could "Cassie" be short for?

"Well, *Cassandra*, what made you finally decide to come? A bit late, isn't it?" The words were tightly spoken, as though Travis Carlyle was holding back some deep resentment.

There was no safe reply, so Joanna made none.

"You couldn't bring yourself to call or write, could you? Just the telegram when it didn't matter anymore. Arne kept making excuses for you. He even . . ." The harsh voice broke off.

In the faint light from the dashboard, Joanna could see strong hands shift and tighten on the steering wheel.

After a moment he continued, bitterness intensifying his voice: "I know you got his last letter. I sent it registered so you'd have to sign for it. But you didn't come like he asked, or even send a postcard. You know what, lady? You've got to be the world's biggest bitch to do what you did to Arne."

"If you think that, why did you come to pick me up at the

bus station?'' The question popped out in spite of her resolve to keep her mouth shut.

Travis turned his head to look at her; she felt him staring at her for a heart-stopping moment before he returned his attention to the road. She wished he would keep it there. The gaping blackness that fell away on one side could be any depth from a few feet to hundreds. She braced herself as he braked and then accelerated around yet another hairpin curve. Her stomach was feeling queasy and she swallowed hard.

''Why? Because, in spite of the fact that you've never bothered to show your face to his friends and family, you are—or were—his wife. I came to get you for his sake. Arne's wife has a right to be at his funeral.''

Joanna felt shock ripple through her, then settle in a hard lump in her uneasy stomach.

''The funeral,'' she asked in a half-strangled voice, ''when is it?''

''Ten o'clock tomorrow morning.''

The words sank in, and Joanna's spirits sank with them. Should she tell him now and ask him to take her back to town? No—they were miles away from the main highway; he might be angry enough to just put her out of the truck and leave her on the road.

He was going on: ''I sent the telegram notifying you of Arne's death as a matter of form. I wasn't even sure if you were still at the same address. I was surprised to get your telegram saying you were coming. Why didn't you come before?'' He shot the question at her like a bullet.

''I . . . couldn't come before. I . . .'' She stuck there, unable to think of anything else she could say.

''You knew he was dying.''

''I never—look here, I . . .''

''Never mind. I don't know why I bothered asking. It doesn't matter now. Arne's gone. But just out of curiosity, what did you do with the money he sent you?''

"The money . . .?"

"Yes, the money! I suppose what he gave you is all gone, so you came to see what's left now that Arne's safely out of the way." His contempt for her was clear. "Do you see yourself as a rich widow, Cassie?"

This had gone far enough. "No!" she said firmly. "Look, mister, I'd better tell you, I'm not—"

"That's right, you're not! The ranch never did belong to Arne, not even in part, but I doubt if he ever told you that. He thought of the ranch as his home, however far away from it he got. So if you married him thinking he was a rich rancher, you were badly mistaken. The ranch is mine." He paused, as if to give her a chance to speak. When she didn't say anything, he went on.

"Like I said, Arne's wife has a right to be at his funeral. You can go through the motions of paying your last respects, and then— as far as I'm concerned—you can get the hell out of here and forget you ever knew anyone by the name of Carlyle."

Joanna swallowed rapidly as the queasy feeling in the pit of her stomach expanded. Travis turned the wheel viciously to negotiate still another wrenching curve, and—"Stop!" she managed to gasp, one hand at her mouth, the other already on the door handle.

Travis braked with a suddenness that threw her against the dashboard. She scrambled hastily out of the truck and gave way to the spasms that emptied the bile from her stomach and left her knees weak and trembling. She became aware of a strong arm supporting her and of a large handkerchief being thrust into her hand. When she motioned that she was ready, he helped her back into the truck where she slumped tiredly, her eyes closed.

Travis slammed the door on her side and walked around to take his own seat. He didn't move to turn on the ignition; instead his fingers tapped a pattern on the steering wheel.

"Are you all right?"

"Yes." Her reply was somewhat muffled as she pressed the handkerchief to her lips.

"Conscience bothering you, maybe?"

"Forget the conscience bit!" she retorted, sitting up. She was mortified by her body's lapse. "If you must drive like a maniac on a road like this, you should provide Dramamine for your passengers!" Almost at once she regretted her outburst. It was dumb to antagonize him further—

"It's beyond me," he said harshly, "how any woman who deserved the name could . . . ." He broke off, expelling the rest in a gust of air from his lungs. "Oh, hell!" he said.

He reached for the ignition, wasting no time in moving back onto the road. Whether out of grudging recognition of her stomach's weakness, or just concern for the interior of his truck, he did keep the speed down.

They had been traveling almost an hour when at last they topped the ridge. Just then the moon broke free from the clouds, and a cold silver light spread over the rain-washed Colorado high country. Etched in the moonlight were dark outlines of spruce and pine; strange rock formations threw weird shadows across the road. Breathtakingly close, the high Rockies rose massively, surrealistically, over all.

But the strange beauty of the scene was wasted on Joanna. She slept, her head finding a resting place in the angle of seat and door. The man beside her stared straight ahead at the moon-bright road.

Joanna opened heavy eyes to find a hard hand shaking her shoulder. Travis was waiting for her in the opened door of the truck, her suitcase already in his hand. Dazedly she pushed away the rug that tangled her legs. He reached out impatiently and took her by the arm. She climbed down, staggering a little as the full force of the cold night wind revived her. There was no time to take her bearings before he was hustling her toward the dark structure that loomed in front of them.

"Watch it!" The warning didn't come in time to save her from stubbing a toe on the first of a set of steps. His hand, firmly gripping her arm, tightened to prevent her from falling. She winced and pressed her lips together.

The house was dark. She heard him swear under his breath, then he had the door open. He held it back with her suitcase, half guiding, half pushing her in ahead of him. A few steps inside, he stopped her.

"Stay put until I get some light," he directed. "The storm has taken out the power line somewhere." In the darkness that surrounded her, she heard the sound of his footsteps receding, leaving her alone.

Joanna began to shiver. She took a tentative step and bumped against a heavy piece of furniture that felt to her groping hand like some kind of table. A peculiar dry, musty scent seemed to come from some source close to her nose.

Suddenly dim light filled the hall from a lamp hanging overhead, and Joanna let out a yelp. She was standing nose to nose with the huge head of an animal. It was a moment before her brain could come up with the reassuring information that the horrifying creature was only the stuffed and mounted head of an ancient elk hanging on the wall above the table she had stumbled into. Both items were covered with dust.

When Travis came through a door at the rear of the large square entrance hall, she glared at him, feeling that her unpleasant fright was all his fault.

He paid no attention, giving her only a cursory glance. Picking up her suitcase, he explained the dim lighting. "I started the generator, but I don't draw on it more than I have to." He moved toward a door on their right. "I'll show you where you can sleep tonight."

Joanna looked after him warily. Only the sound of Travis' voice had broken the silence of the big house. It was beginning to look like she had guessed wrong about Travis being married. Whom had he meant by "we," then?

Uneasy at the growing conviction that she was alone with a strange man in an empty house, Joanna slowly followed the rancher into a living room of massive proportions. A ceiling-hung lamp in one corner provided limited lighting. A natural stone fireplace extended over most of one wall, its square firebox now blackened and cold. Bulky, old-fashioned furniture crowded the room.

"Cassie!"

An impatient call caused her to hurry after Travis, who had passed through a door on the far side. Stepping into the hallway of what appeared to be another wing, Joanna saw Travis waiting farther down near an open door. He reached inside and flicked a switch, then waited for her to enter.

The room was a small bedroom, and its Spartan simplicity together with his aloof expression were enough to dispel the uneasy thoughts that had begun to gather in her mind. The chaste narrow bed was topped with a handmade faded quilt. There was a chair, a chest of drawers, and a dressing table with a small mirror hanging above it. The two windows on one side were uncurtained and reflected their images back starkly. Joanna hugged her arms across her chest to subdue another bout of shivering.

Travis set the suitcase down by the bed. "I just turned the furnace on again; it'll be a few minutes before it warms up in here." He gestured toward the register set low in one wall, and Joanna moved nearer to the warm air flowing from the grilled opening. She jumped a little when he spoke again.

"The bathroom is the next door down the hall. Do you want anything to eat before you go to bed?"

Unwilling to ask him for anything, Joanna shook her head. "I'm all right, thanks," she said huskily.

Travis stepped past her to the door. With one hand on the doorknob, he paused, frowning. His eyes swept over her clinically. "I'll bring you a hot drink. You look like you need one." He left, closing the door behind him.

After a long moment, Joanna removed her raincoat, hanging it in the small closet. The house was as old-fashioned as the furniture, she judged; built in the days before large wardrobes had been considered necessary. Grimacing at her reflection in the mirror, she pulled the limp scarf from her head and let it fall on the dressing table. Her legs felt a bit wobbly and she sat down on the edge of the bed. What a relief to kick off her shoes! She ran her hands through her hair, massaging her head to relieve the tension.

She blinked as the overhead light brightened suddenly, taking away the oppressive gloom.

Travis tapped on the door and entered, carrying a steaming mug. ''I put some brandy in it. I thought . . .'' He stopped, staring at her with unconcealed surprise.

A mass of dark disheveled hair fell in a cloud about Joanna's face, pale now with weariness. Her eyes were a glittering blue, startling to anyone seeing them clearly for the first time. Without the concealing scarf that had been tied so tightly under her chin, the sharply defined bones of her face gave her a look that was peculiarly arresting. Intelligence shone from the blue eyes. A mobile mouth indented at the corners hinted at a capacity for laughter. Her figure was slender, beautifully proportioned; her breasts, partially revealed by the deep slash of her neckline, were rounded and firm. Travis was by no means the first man in Joanna's life to stand temporarily bemused by her striking, very feminine attractions. Even so, her bare toes curled self-consciously as his glance traveled the length of her and back again.

His gray eyes narrowed on the dress she was wearing. Closefitting, made of a clinging coral fabric, it was the kind of dress a woman would wear on a very special date, not on a long journey into the mountains by bus and truck.

It wasn't until she reached out to take the mug from him that he seemed to realize he was still holding it. Joanna saw him gazing at her ringless left hand.

"Thank you, Mr. Carlyle." She wrapped her fingers around the cup's warmth and watched him warily.

"I'll call you in the morning. It'll be early." His voice rasped, and his face hardened against her again. He turned abruptly on his heel and left the room, not bothering to say good night.

It was several moments before she remembered the drink in her hands. Hot, milky, and laced with good brandy, it was delicious and she savored every reviving drop. Finished, she set the empty cup on the dressing table and resisted the desire to crawl into the bed just as she was.

She rose with an effort and lifted the suitcase onto the foot of the bed. The manila envelope containing the lease options was there, on top, just where she had thrown it. She slipped the envelope out of sight under the few garments in the hastily packed suitcase and thought with regret of the extensive wardrobe she had abandoned in Denver. Taking out her nightgown, she closed the case and set it aside, ready for a quick departure in the morning if it proved necessary.

She would have to try calling Donovan again. With the coral dress half unzipped, Joanna paused. After a moment's thought, she discarded the notion of creeping around the house looking for a telephone. That would be pushing her luck for sure. Perhaps she'd have a chance in the morning. If she didn't get thrown out first.

The air had lost its chill, but she was glad to slip beneath the covers. As she snuggled into the soft feather pillow Joanna thought of the bus station and the hard seat she had figured would be her bed for the night. She couldn't quite find it in herself to regret the change. Risky as her situation might be, at least she could be grateful for a good night's sleep in the bed meant for the missing Cassie.

Why hadn't Cassie been on the bus, after sending that telegram? Travis sure had a bad opinion of her; it hadn't been pleasant being on the receiving end of his scathing looks and words. Though he'd been kind, too, almost in spite of himself. Giving her the rug in the cold truck, holding her up when she was sick on the road . . . the hot drink . . . She slipped into the half-world of sleep and dreamed of a hard masculine face that softened and grew tender. . . .

Chapter Two

"Cassie!" Impatience roughened the masculine voice that summoned her back from dream-filled sleep.

Joanna muttered a response, then she heard the sound of retreating footsteps. For a moment she stared blankly around, dazzled by the morning sunlight streaming into the plain little room. She groaned and burrowed under the bedcovers. Memories of the night before crowded in, none of them welcome. After a moment she yawned and sat up. There was no help for it. She had to face the facts of her situation and decide what to do.

One, she simply couldn't afford to let Gerald get any hint of where she was. Two, she had walked into a touchy situation on the Carlyle ranch, and getting out of it might not be easy.

A tingling sensation rippled up the back of her neck, and Joanna reached up a hand to rub the tingle away. That was how she'd felt that time skiing in Squaw Valley tackling the advanced slope a couple of lessons sooner than her instructor had advised. She'd made it okay that time, hadn't she?

She'd taken a spill and almost hit a tree, but the exhilarating run had been worth it. Maybe there was more of her father's gambling instinct in her than she'd realized. He'd always been willing to take risks when high stakes were involved.

It had been some time since she'd thought of her father. She had been eleven years old when he had left her in foster care and gone off on his own, a year after her mother had died. For a while she'd hoped he would come back for her. Until the day the social worker had told her, as kindly as she could, that he had been found shot dead in a motel room, his body lying on the cards that had made up his last hand of poker.

Joanna stirred restlessly. Maybe she had a little too much of her father in her. Heaven knew she was in a tight spot now. Whether she liked it or not, it appeared to be the lesser of two evils to go on as Cassie for a short while, even if it proved to be embarrassing. Better that than to end up hospitalized or worse, if Gerald's men found her.

She would take it one step at a time; keep her mouth shut as much as possible, and hope she'd get through somehow. Impatiently she thrust back the covers, dug her makeup kit out of her purse, and made her way to the bathroom.

The bathroom contained a lingering aroma of tangy after-shave, and Joanna sniffed appreciatively. A damp towel was crumpled on the hamper near the still-steamy shower, and a brief disturbing vision of Travis Carlyle naked under streaming water flashed through her mind. She placed her makeup bag next to his shaving kit on the counter by the hand basin. Sharing a stranger's bathroom felt almost illicitly intimate.

After a quick shower, Joanna studied her reflection in the mirror above the basin. Her face looked too angular, and her hair was a mess. She felt somewhat better after brushing her teeth and putting a moisturizer on her skin. Even her hair didn't look too bad after she brushed the tangles out. She cautiously looked both ways outside the bathroom door before scampering back to the bedroom wrapped in a towel. Unfortunately her robe had been left behind in Denver.

She dressed in a navy wool pantsuit and a white blouse, hoping the wrinkles would fall out quickly. It was the only thing she had to wear except jeans or the coral dress. She spared a thought for the unmade bed, then shrugged and stepped out into the hall.

There were other doors farther down; one stood ajar and she glimpsed part of an ornately carved four-poster. She glanced out the windows that lined the hallway along one side. A straggling garden filled the space between the wing she was in and another one that completed the U-shaped building.

She saw a matching door on the far side of the main entrance hall. Joanna heard the muffled sound of male voices; taking a deep breath, she opened the door. As expected, she found herself in the other wing. The near end of the long room she entered was almost bare of furnishings. On one side was a wide, deep bay window, which, like all the other windows she had seen, was curtainless. At the other end of the room was a kitchen area, and sitting at a square table near the stove were Travis and an older man. They were eating breakfast. Both were dressed in suits and ties.

They looked around as she walked toward them. Travis' eyes narrowed. His expression told her he didn't think a wrinkled trouser outfit was the proper garb for a widow attending her husband's funeral. She waited for a sarcastic comment, but his mouth maintained its straight line. The coffee cup in his hand was brought down on the table with a thump; his booted foot came out and hooked the rung of the empty chair nearest him, pushing it out from the table.

"Your breakfast is on the back of the stove. Help yourself."

Joanna shrugged. She was in no position to complain, however rude his manners. At least he had fixed her something to eat. She walked over to the stove and picked up the plate, which was filled with eggs, bacon, and toast. She put it on the table and sat down. There was a jar with some battered silverware in the middle of the table, and she took a fork from it.

The other man tilted his head and finished his coffee in one swallow. Joanna guessed his age to be somewhere in the late fifties. His face was weathered; his hands showed the scars of years of rough work. Since Travis hadn't troubled to introduce them, did that mean she was supposed to know who he was?

Travis apparently decided some kind of introduction was called for, after all. "Arne probably told you about Barney. Barney Olaffson, meet Cassie Carlyle. She does exist after all, just like Arne said."

Joanna ignored the sarcasm and acknowledged the mumbled greeting of the older man. She wondered what Cassie had been told about Barney. If Cassie was a Carlyle, then Arne must have been Travis' brother, or maybe a cousin.

When Travis glanced impatiently at her untouched plate, she poked at her egg with her fork. To one accustomed to fruit, toast, and coffee in the morning, this man-sized breakfast was daunting. Looking up, she caught Barney staring covertly at her. His gaze immediately shifted, and he got up from the table, a dull flush rising under his tanned skin.

"I'll bring the truck around, Trav," he said gruffly. He left via the screen door at the rear of the kitchen.

Lowering her eyes to her plate, Joanna forced herself to take a bite of egg, ignoring the silent man at her side. The second bite took no effort at all; the food was tasty and she began to eat with real appreciation. How long *had* it been since her last meal?

A cup of hot coffee was pushed in front of her. She looked up to see Travis reaching with one long arm to replace the pot on the stove behind him. The movement caused the front of his suit jacket to fall open, and her eyes were drawn to his muscled torso, which narrowed into a lean, supple waist. She could see the shadow of dark body hair through the fabric of his shirt; more of the same dusted the backs of his hands and disappeared beneath the cuffs of his dress shirt. That prickling awareness disturbed the back of her neck again.

She looked away quickly and picked up her cup in both hands. She propped her elbows on the table; if manners were going by the board, she might as well be comfortable. After a moment, she glanced at him again, to find he was examining her with clinical detachment.

"Is there something wrong with the way I look?" Her chin tilted upward as she spoke.

"No, you've done the look very well, I think." His voice was sardonic. "Pale cheeks, no color on your mouth; you've even got faint circles under your eyes. You look the part of a bereaved widow, all right. Except for a wedding ring. What happened? Did you get rid of it as soon as you heard you were a widow? Or did the wedding take place in too much of a hurry to bother with one?"

Automatically the fingers of her right hand touched the bare third finger of her left hand. Her wit failed to come up with a response; she kept her eyes on his face. At close quarters, she saw the lines of strain around his mouth and eyes, making it hard to tell his age. Maybe about thirty, she guessed. Intuitively she knew he wasn't nearly as hard and unfeeling as she had thought.

Impulsively she said, "Look, Mr. Carlyle, I think I made a mistake coming here. I don't know Arne's family and friends, and I really don't want to hurt anybody. Maybe it would be better if I don't intrude at the services today." She forced herself to meet his eyes, but she couldn't fathom his expression as he looked at her for a long moment.

His gaze shifted to his watch, and he stood up. "You let Arne down when he was alive," he said flatly. "It's up to you if you do it again today. Barney and I are leaving in five minutes.'' He didn't look at her as he started toward the door.

"Travis . . ."

He looked back, his face closed.

Awkwardly she said, "I'm sorry. I guess you don't believe that, but I am."

His expression didn't change. "Are you?" The screen door swung to behind him.

With his departure the kitchen seemed very quiet. Joanna felt uncharacteristically depressed. Her appetite gone, she rose and carried their plates and cups to the sink. Her gaze was drawn to the view outside the window over the sink. Stretches of grassland blended with tree-studded outcroppings on the plateau, which was sheltered by the nearby peaks of the Rockies. The sun's rays had begun to change from shadowed purple to gold and misty gray. A small sigh escaped her. If only she felt some of that serenity inside herself . . . Squaring her shoulders, she went outside.

By the time they arrived at the mountain chapel where the funeral was to be held, there was a dew of nervous perspiration on her forehead and upper lip. She wiped it off with her handkerchief before Barney helped her down out of the truck. They entered the chapel's reception area and a sea of faces turned to stare. Heads bent toward each other, and Joanna heard the whispering over the plaintive sound of an organ. Her eyes were drawn to the flower-banked area in front of the congregation where a closed casket rested. She took a firm grasp on Travis' arm. He stiffened but allowed her hand to stay where it was. A soberly dressed man greeted Travis quietly, then led them to a small alcove on one side, slightly separated from the rest. After a moment, the organ ceased playing, and the service began.

Joanna kept her eyes fixed on the minister as he began to speak. His words were sincere, his voice deep with feeling as he talked about Arne Carlyle. She learned that Arne was the adopted son of Travis' parents and that he had spent the past several years in Denver, working for the state as a social worker. A humane, caring man emerged from the picture drawn by the minister. What would a man like that have thought of her impersonating his wife? she wondered. Guilt oppressed her, and she didn't dare look at Travis. She was much too aware of the tight control he was exerting on himself, as he sat rigidly next to her.

" . . . his marriage to Cassandra, in Denver, a short while ago," the minister was saying. He went on to an obscure exhortation that amounted to a plea for understanding and forgiveness, though it was not put in quite those terms. His words fell on mostly deaf ears, however. Joanna's face burned at the expressions of disapproval and hostility she received as those sitting close to the alcove craned their necks to look at her. She began to feel that the one thing worse than being an impostor was to be the real Cassie. By the time the service ended, she felt drained.

The final graveside words were spoken in a cemetery that dated back to pioneer days. Standing between Travis and Barney, Joanna could see pitted, mossy headstones that bore dates going back into the previous century. The Carlyle plot contained some of the earliest. Travis' parents, Sarah and Bradford Carlyle, were buried side by side next to the newly dug grave for Arne. Joanna glanced upward at Travis and saw the jerky movement of a muscle on one side of his stiffly held face.

Afterward, most of the farmers and ranchers and their families stopped to speak briefly to Travis and Barney. Joanna received a few stiff nods and perfunctory words of condolence, but it was clear most of the community had already formed negative opinions about the missing Cassie.

An older man, tall and sunburned under his Stetson hat, came up to Travis, accompanied by two women. After exchanging a few words, Travis introduced them to Joanna.

"Cassie, this is John and Maureen Temple and their

daughter, Sally. The Temples knew Arne well. Their ranch borders ours on the east.''

''How . . . do you do.'' Joanna found it necessary to clear her throat as her voice emerged in husky syllables. The strain of maintaining her imposture was beginning to tell on her. She prayed inwardly for an end to this ordeal so they could leave.

Mrs. Temple gave Joanna a short nod and a murmured greeting, but her daughter's hostility was evident in her silence. About seventeen, the girl was rather plain, with the height and angularity of her father's physique. When Mr. Temple prodded her, Sally muttered a grudging ''Hello.'' Her eyes flickered from Joanna to Travis. Her hand went out to touch Travis' arm, and her eyes softened.

''I'm so sorry about Arne,'' she said earnestly.

''We're all going to miss him, Travis,'' John Temple added. ''You and Barney especially, I know.''

His daughter cast a scornful look at Joanna. ''*She* won't, I bet,'' she muttered insolently.

''Sally!'' her father exclaimed.

''Well, we all know she didn't care anything about Arne. She made that plain enough. I don't see any tears on *her* face.''

''That's enough, Sally,'' her mother reproved. ''Remember what Arne said.''

''Sure, I remember. 'She's going to need friends,' he said. Well, she doesn't look to me like she needs anything.''

''Please excuse Sally's rudeness, Cassie.'' Red with embarrassment, John Temple clamped a hand on Sally's arm. ''I think we'd better be getting along. Travis, I'll give you a call later.'' He kept his grip on his daughter's elbow as he hustled the two women away.

Her own cheeks a vivid color, Joanna turned to find herself under the scrutiny of a short middle-aged woman.

''Never mind, dear,'' the woman said. Half a head

shorter than Joanna, she was almost twice as broad. Her head tipped to one side appraisingly.

"So you're Arne's Cassie," she said, not bothering to speak in lowered tones as most of the others had. "You're taller than I expected. He called you a little bit of a thing, you know. And you'd think he'd have mentioned those eyes. Goodness me, they're just the color of my prize asters. Never mind what Sally said, dear. She's young, yet, but she'll learn."

Joanna blinked at the sudden veering of the woman's remarks. Warily she accepted the plump work-toughened hand held out to her. No one else had offered to shake hands with her.

"Maggie Puldowski's the name, dear. And this's my husband, George." Maggie reached out and tugged the arm of the stocky farmer who was clasping Travis' hand in a hard grip of wordless sympathy. The kindly-faced man nodded gravely at Joanna but didn't speak.

"Trav, you know how sorry we are." Sincerity rang in Maggie's booming voice. Silent condolence was clearly not her way. She reached out to grasp Travis' hand, looking up at him with a furrowed brow. "Seems like only yesterday when Sarah and Brad took that little scamp in. And now he's gone."

Her keen black eyes subjected Joanna to further scrutiny. "This girl will be a help to you, Trav. She looks like she's got good stuff in her."

Joanna smiled at her unexpected champion, then glanced at Travis' frowning face.

"Cassie won't be staying, Maggie."

"Is that right, Cassie?"

"Well, I . . . I hadn't planned . . ." Joanna stammered, not ready to deal with the question in public.

"Now, don't you let people's attitudes put you off." Maggie made a dismissing gesture toward the slowly dispersing crowd. The Temples were no longer in view.

"Some folks who knew Arne are upset 'cause they don't understand a few things. They forget that Arne Carlyle never did do just what you expected him to. If he picked you, he picked you for a good reason, and that's good enough for us, isn't that right, George?"

Again her husband nodded gravely, running blunt fingers around the brim of the weather-stained Stetson he held in his hands. His wife continued, unabashed by Travis' frown.

"Trav, don't you let this girl get away just yet. Have her stick around and get to know us. We're not so bad; just a little standoffish at times." Nodding kindly at the three of them, Maggie turned away with her husband toward a battered old Chevrolet sedan.

"Let's go," Travis said brusquely. Maggie's frank remarks hung between them. His silence on the question of her staying was just as eloquent as a direct order to leave.

Very little was said on the way back to the ranch. Barney and Travis exchanged a few words about the mare that had foaled the day before. When they arrived at the ranch, Travis followed the drive around to the kitchen wing and stopped the truck close to the veranda entrance. Barney disappeared in the direction of the barn as if glad to get away. Travis stalked to the rear of the truck and removed a hamper that had been carefully wedged in. He carried it inside and set it down on the table.

"The neighbors sent some food over. Eat, if you're hungry. Barney and I have things to take care of outside." Travis left the kitchen through a door on the garden side, pulling his tie loose as he strode across to the bedroom wing.

Now what? Joanna wondered. He hadn't said anything more about her leaving—he had hardly looked at her, and that was something she wasn't used to. Men usually looked at her a lot. Immediately she felt ashamed; what did she expect? The man had just seen his adopted brother buried. And he thought she was a woman he had cause to hate. If circumstances were different, she would have liked to get to know him, to learn what kind of man was behind that stark but interesting face.

He had the face of a man capable of strong passion. A woman who found herself on the receiving end of that passion might get more than she bargained for, though. This house, and Travis himself, bore the marks of a man who had been alone too long.

Frowning thoughtfully, she opened the hamper. She wasn't hungry, but some of the food might need to go in the refrigerator.

The food was both plain and appetizing. Fried chicken, vegetable casseroles, potato salad, a large luscious-looking apple pie. There was something to be said for living in a small community. Your neighbors cared enough to make sure you didn't go hungry in times of personal loss and stress.

The breakfast things were still in the sink, so she decided to clear them up. Obviously no one else was going to. Through the window over the sink she saw Travis, once again in his work clothes, striding away from the house toward the barn. Her hands slowed and she put down the scouring pad she was using on the skillet.

Now that she was alone in the house, she should call Donovan. Explaining to the old man what had happened was not going to be easy. It might be difficult to track him down, too. That would be one more thing she owed Travis: toll charges on his telephone bill. Well, it couldn't be helped. She looked around the kitchen. What could she do in return? Scrub the floors or wash the windows, she mused vaguely. The long room was too cluttered near the cooking area and too bare in the front part. It badly needed rearranging. The phone call to Donovan receded in urgency as she speculated about Travis and his rather Spartan home.

Whatever talents Travis had, they didn't include home-making. Why wasn't he married? Such a good-looking, virile man must have the local women falling all over themselves for the opportunity of sharing his bed. Which might be the reason he wasn't married, she thought cynically.

Joanna wandered through the house looking around. She had never been in a home that looked like it dated back to pioneer days. As nearly as she could tell, the building had been added to a section at a time. The kitchen wing was oldest, probably. The additions must mean that at one time the Carlyles were a large family. What had happened to them all? Barney seemed to be the nearest thing to a family that Travis had left. But she had gathered from comments overheard that morning that Barney worked as a ranch hand for Travis.

She entered the bedroom wing, and giving way to curiosity, investigated all the rooms. There were no linens on any of the beds except the one she had slept in and the four-poster in the last and largest of the rooms.

She went in for a closer look. Travis' room, of course. His sheepskin jacket was hanging behind a half-opened closet door. The room was crowded but tidy. A big rolltop desk filled one corner. Files were stacked on the floor near the desk and on a nearby chest of drawers. The bed was made of solid oak with ornately turned posts as tall as she was. Unusually large for an antique bed, she thought. That mattress must be a queen size at least, probably custom-made.

Absently she ran her hand over the faded quilt that covered the bed, wondering about the careful needlewoman who had so painstakingly pieced the pattern together. There was a bookshelf near the bed, and she scanned the titles: a few classics, some fairly recent best-sellers, books on animal husbandry and technical subjects. A clock on one of the shelves reminded her of the passing time, and she remembered she still had to call Donovan.

There was a telephone on the small bedside chest, so she

sat on the edge of the bed and picked up the receiver. She had no success at the first two numbers she tried. Directory Assistance gave her a couple of other numbers that were possibilities.

"Donovan might be at Lucy's, Joanna," said the cook at Joe's Café. "Say, some guys were in here asking where you were. What's up?"

Joanna put him off with a vague answer and hung up. She paused, frowning. If Gerald had gone after Donovan, he might hurt him trying to find out where the papers were. Maybe she hadn't done her friend a favor after all . . .

She had first met Donovan when he came to see Gerald about investing money in some oil lease options Donovan had. Joanna had liked his free-spirited manner and captivating yarns right away, and after a few more visits, his integrity and kind heart had won her respect. He had invited her to meet some of his friends, and she learned firsthand what oil prospecting was like before high-tech and astronomical development costs had edged out the shoestring operators. Over tankards of foaming beer, she was treated to tales of boom times and bust times, of fortunes lost and friends made and not forgotten. Joanna enjoyed a feeling of acceptance and welcome that she had encountered all too seldom in her life. It was almost like being part of a family. And in a way, Donovan was like the father she had lost so long ago.

She dialed the next number on her list—Lucy's—a bar that was a favorite hangout of some of the oil workers and oldtimers like Donovan. She heaved a sigh of relief when she heard his scratchy voice.

"Joanna? Where in tarnation are you, girl? Are you all right? What'd you want to go taking those options away from Lasker for? He's awful mad, honey, and he's looking for you."

She laughed ruefully. "Don't jump on me, Donovan. I didn't mean to make such a mess of things. It's just that it made me so mad when he stole those leases from you—well, I couldn't let him get away with it, could I? Not when I saw the chance to get them back. The only thing is, I didn't figure on him finding out it was me who took them.''

"It was my own fault he got them away from me. I figured Lasker for a sharp operator the first time I ever come into his office. I just didn't figure *how* sharp. But I didn't mean for you to get yourself involved, Joanna. Are you okay?''

"I'm fine, Donovan, but now I'm afraid I've just made a lot of trouble for you. Did Gerald give you a hard time?''

"We had a bit of a go-round till he found I didn't know where you was, then he laid off me. There's a couple fellers followin' me around wherever I go now.'' His voice became muffled, as though he were bent over the mouthpiece of the telephone. "You got them papers with you?''

"Yes, I was going to—''

"Listen, honey, I appreciate what you were tryin' to do for me, but I sure wish you hadn't got yourself on the wrong side of Lasker. I'd rather lose the whole shootin' match than see you get hurt. He's mean when he's riled.''

"Well, it's too late now; I've already done it. Things just didn't go quite as I expected them to. It might be a good idea to let things cool down before I call you again, then we can make some kind of arrangements about the papers.''

"That'd be best,'' he agreed. A burst of laughter came from the background in the bar. "Look, I gotta hang up. Those guys are coming in; I think they seen me talking on the phone.''

Joanna stifled a protest as the connection was broken. Putting the receiver down, she chewed her lower lip worriedly. Gerald's men were watching the old man too closely. She wouldn't dare send the papers to him or even try to call again soon.

A sound from the hall made her turn. Travis was standing in the doorway, his eyes narrowed with suspicion. Her heart lurched unpleasantly. How much had he heard? She rose slowly from the bed, unable to look away from his grim face.

Travis stepped inside the room and leaned against the doorframe, folding his arms across his chest. "You've made yourself at home, I see," he said.

"I wanted to use the phone."

His eyebrows went up. "Something wrong with the phone in the kitchen?"

Joanna flushed. "Actually I was just looking around the house. I came in here to see this old bed, and then I just used your phone because it was handy." Her eyes followed the direction of his gaze to the desk. "I wasn't snooping around in your papers, if that's what you're thinking."

He moved to the desk and checked the loose papers lying there. "Unless you're interested in cattle-breeding records, it wouldn't do you much good if you *were* snooping." He leaned his tall frame against the desk with a casualness that was at odds with the aggressive thrust of his jaw. "I came back to talk to you."

"Oh?" Joanna unconsciously raised a hand and tucked a stray wave of hair behind her ear. "What about?"

"Your plans to leave, of course."

The quickened rise and fall of her breasts beneath the white blouse gave away the fact she was not as calm as she pretended. She had taken off her navy jacket to do the dishes, and now she felt underdressed as he looked her over coolly.

"I do plan to leave," she began reluctantly, "but . . ."

"You're a little short on cash?"

"Yes." She hated to make the admission, but there was no point in lying about it.

"So you're not able to move on without help," he concluded.

"That's right. I'd leave if I could, but until I can earn it, I don't have the price of my fare."

"And you want a loan, right?" A thought seemed to occur to him. "You wouldn't be pregnant, by any chance?"

"No! To both questions!"

"From the sound of that telephone conversation, you didn't do as well as you expected here, did you? What was that about needing to wait till things cooled down?"

Joanna's eyes sped to his. Of course he'd heard that last part of the conversation. "It was nothing to do with you, I promise you that," she declared, hoping the answer would satisfy him.

The cynical expression that came into his eyes told her he had little faith in her promise. Watching for her reaction, he said, "Arne spent a lot of time in the city. But he used to talk about his work when he came home. He told us he came across a lot of hard-luck people. Borderline criminals, prostitutes, addicts, that sort of thing." His next words were deliberately insulting: "Arne told me you were one of his cases."

She met his look squarely. "Really? What am I supposed to do now? Confess to being a prostitute or an addict? I'm not wanted by the police, if that's what's worrying you." Mentally she crossed her fingers, hoping that last part was true; she didn't think Gerald would call in the law.

"You could be more forthcoming about yourself." He waited, giving her an opportunity to comment. When her only answer was to hunch her shoulders and look away, he smiled, unpleasantly. "I believe I could make a few assumptions about you and be right on target," he said.

"Such as?"

"Such as, you were in a jam, you gave Arne some song and dance that made him take pity on you, and you tricked a sick man into marrying you for reasons of your own, probably shady."

"Arne never told you that," she objected, her temper rising. It was becoming difficult to keep her own identity and pride separate from Cassie's.

"Why did Arne marry you? You're not sick, you're dressed too well to be needy, and you're too damn beautiful to have trouble finding a man to take care of you." He looked her over insultingly, taking his time. There was something hot and scornful in the hardness of his gaze. "Don't tell me he married you for love, because Arne wouldn't do that to a woman he loved—leave her a widow before the ink was dry on the marriage license. He knew he could die anytime."

"What was wrong with him?" she asked bluntly. No one had mentioned it at the funeral.

Scorn curled his lips. "Don't tell me you didn't know about his heart condition." When she didn't reply, he laughed shortly. "You make a bad actress, Cassie. Why bother trying to pretend?"

"Obviously you've made up your mind about me, so why should I try to change it?"

He pondered, frowning. "Whatever the circumstances, he did marry you. When he got ill and came home without you, he said you'd come on your own. 'When she's ready,' he said. He wouldn't let me go after you, said it might scare you off. What kind of thing is that to say about a new bride? When I asked him why, he put me off. Just kept saying wait and see."

Joanna twined her fingers together to keep them from fidgeting. She looked toward the door. He didn't miss the direction of her glance or fail to put his own interpretation on it.

"Anxious to leave? I'll get Barney to take you into town, and you can have enough money to get to Denver or wherever else you want to go. For Arne's sake, not yours," he added when her eyes flashed back to meet his steady gaze.

"I'm not asking for any favors," Joanna told him proudly. "I don't take something for nothing, whatever you think to the contrary."

"It doesn't look like you're in a position to do anything else."

"I could work to earn what I need. Here at the ranch."

His mouth curved satirically. "You mean you're offering to punch cattle? I didn't know city women got that kind of training."

Joanna gave him a withering look and walked over to the bureau. She wiped a finger across the surface and held it out for him to see the smear of dust.

"There's plenty to do around here that should be worth the cost of a bus ticket to Cheyenne and pay for my keep as well. It shouldn't take more than about a week."

There was a long pause before Travis replied. "A week can be a long time," he murmured slowly, his expression enigmatic. "You think you could stick to honest work that long?"

"Of course." She ignored the slur. If she took offense at every gibe he made at her expense, she'd only give him the satisfaction of seeing her lose her temper, an advantage she didn't want him to have.

"It might be worth it, at that. Just to watch you try. Maybe it'll help you think twice next time you decide to take on a gullible husband."

"So is it a deal or not?" she challenged, and saw a spark flash in his eyes.

It was impossible to tell from his expression what he was really thinking. Whatever emotion had flashed from him just then was not indifference, she was certain.

"We'll try it." His voice made her jump. "The ranch work has fallen behind. Barney and I will be working flat out the next couple of weeks. It could even be useful, not having to stop and cook or do the laundry. Can you cook?"

"Sure." She didn't exactly enjoy it, but she could cook. There had been times when her survival in foster homes had depended on it.

"You can start with supper tonight, then," he said. "Just

put out the things Maggie sent over. That'll give you time to get your bearings in the kitchen.''

She started to leave and he stopped her. ''Just one thing. I'd suggest you use the kitchen phone if you want to call your friends. Stay out of my bedroom from now on.''

''No problem,'' Joanna replied, her color high. She shut the door harder than she intended to on her way out.

Chapter Three

Joanna gave a last swipe with the polishing cloth across an expanse of gleaming mahogany dark with age and use. The rich brown wood had responded beautifully to furniture oil and hand rubbing. Stepping back, she admired the dignity the heavy table gave to the main hallway.

When her eyes fell on the elkhead mounted above, however, she grimaced with distaste. The glassy eyes were aloof, and the mouth seemed to curl with disdain. Impishly she stuck out her tongue. That curled mouth reminded her of Travis at his most disapproving, and she couldn't resist. Not that she'd seen much of Travis lately. He and Barney were working long, hard hours to make up for time lost during the previous month. The reason for the lost time was never discussed, at least not in front of Joanna, but she guessed that it had something to do with Arne's illness.

The week she had thought would be sufficient to earn her expenses and bus fare was almost over. She had been as busy as the men, having hot meals ready for them whenever they came in, plus catching up on general housekeeping chores and tackling a mountain of laundry.

She smiled with satisfaction. If Travis had expected her to cry "uncle" after a few days of hard work and early hours, well, by this time he had learned different. Without an alarm clock, she was unable to beat Travis by getting up earlier than he did, but the sound of his boots as he strode past her door each morning woke her up just as effectively. So far she had managed to join him in the kitchen, dressed in her jeans and T-shirt, by the time he was pouring his first cup of coffee. Barney usually came in, yawning, about the time she had the bacon and eggs ready to turn out onto plates. Not until they had left for the day's work did she allow herself to drop her attitude of calm efficiency and sit back down at the table, her eyes drooping sleepily, to enjoy the extra cup of coffee it took to really get her going so early in the day.

It seemed strange, at first, to live alone in a house with an attractive man who hardly ever spoke to her, and then only in monosyllables. She was careful to time her baths or showers when she knew Travis wouldn't be about. And, since he took his own showers while she was putting supper on the table, there was no conflict. Only once had they met in the hallway when, having forgotten to brush her teeth, she had slipped out in her nightgown to remedy her oversight. Travis, dressed to go out in slacks and a sweater under his sheepskin jacket, had stopped short. His eyes swept over her, once—then he brushed quickly past her. She rubbed her bare arms, feeling almost scorched by that one raking glance. It was very late before he returned that night; half awake, she heard his footsteps as he hesitated outside her door, then went on to his room, leaving her wondering where he had been and what had stopped him from trying the handle of her door.

Except for that one incident, Travis seemed oblivious of her presence just down the hallway. That was a relief, of course, but it left her somewhat piqued that she made so little impression on him.

Barney, she learned, had his own cabin elsewhere on the property and only came to the big house for his meals and for company. After supper, the men usually talked about ranch affairs, watched a television program, or played a game of chess. Sometimes, as she read the newspaper or one of the farming journals that seemed to be the only magazines Travis subscribed to, Joanna would look up and watch them, envying their easy companionship. It was hard not to feel lonely, but the less she was included in their conversation the safer it was for her, so she couldn't complain just because "Cassie" was still clearly on probation.

So what was she doing, standing here making faces at a stuffed elkhead? She'd let herself get housebound, that was all. What she needed was a breath of fresh air! She stepped outside onto the veranda and tugged at her close-fitting top to let the air reach her perspiring skin. The late summer days were still hot; only in the early morning and late evening did the chill from the high, snow-covered mountains make itself felt.

A frown creased her brow. Jeans and T-shirts were enough for now, but she would need something less casual to wear while she looked for work in Cheyenne or elsewhere. Maybe she could make a deal with Travis to stay a little longer and get more of a stake together, if he could bring himself to acknowledge the value of her efforts in his home. She'd feel safer here than on public view in a diner somewhere, worrying about every customer who came in for a sandwich, wondering if they were working for Gerald.

A movement at her feet caused her to look down. The barn cats, a calico and a black and white tabby, were twining around her feet. She stooped to pet them.

"Hello there, Curly. Hi, Spats. What're you two doing? Travis will be after you if he catches you over here again."

Spats, the black and white, meowed questioningly, and

she scolded him. "That cream you got from me yesterday morning was a one-shot deal because I didn't know any better—how was I supposed to know house-fed cats won't bother to catch mice?"

She scratched his ears, and Spats purred back at her. "What's the action like out in the barn, boys? Maybe I should go see, now that I've got the house fixed up." Her spirits rising, she brushed her hands along her thighs and went down the steps of the veranda toward the barn.

Sawdust was soft underfoot as she stepped through the big doors. The barn housed several horses as well as a great deal of equipment, feed, and hay. A whuffling sound called her attention to a large stall on one side, and she saw a horse looking anxiously her way. She walked closer and saw the foal. Why, this must be the mare that foaled the day she arrived! The new baby stood on spindly legs, as close to its mother as possible, wearing such a brightly inquiring look that Joanna laughed.

"You darling," she crooned. "Come closer, sweetheart, I won't hurt you. Let me get a look at you." She extended her fingers to the youngster and made a kissing sound with her lips.

Someone behind her giggled and she heard Sally Temple's young voice. "You're not going to let *her* take care of the horses, are you, Travis? I thought she'd never been on a ranch before."

Joanna swung around to see Travis, dressed in his usual jeans and workshirt and wearing his sweat-stained Stetson hat. Sally was likewise dressed in jeans and shirt, but her jeans were carefully faded designer ones, and her pink shirt was crisply new. She stared at Joanna with poorly concealed antagonism.

"What do you think of our newest addition?" Travis ignored Sally's dig and addressed Joanna, causing her eyebrows to arch in surprise. He came over to lean on the front of the horse box. Sally's lip thrust out in a pout, and she plumped down on a nearby bale of straw.

"He's beautiful." Joanna smiled at them both, her eyes sparkling. "Or should I say she?"

"Huh. Can't even tell the difference, can you?" Sally muttered scornfully.

Travis favored Sally with a quelling look before answering Joanna. "She's a filly. For a while we weren't sure she'd make it, or Belle either."

Joanna's eyes followed the prancing movements of the foal as the mare, Belle, bent her neck protectively over her offspring. "I'm so glad you saved her. Did you have to call in a veterinarian?"

"Travis is practically a vet himself, didn't you know that?" Sally was indignant. "Folks call on him for help as much as they do the regular vet. Travis studied it in college and everything."

"Really? But you didn't finish training to become a veterinarian?" Joanna asked Travis curiously.

"I studied to become a better rancher, not to become a vet. I took the training I thought would come in most handy." Travis opened the gate and went inside the box. He ran a practiced hand over the mare and looked critically at the foal.

With gentle hands, he guided the filly up to the low barrier. Belle rolled her eyes nervously, not very pleased at all the attention her youngster was getting. "Want to say howdy? You can touch her if you like."

Still surprised at the unexpected thaw in Travis' manner, Joanna reached over and carefully touched the silky brown hide. Her fingers caressed the rounded cheek and jaw, the curving slender neck. But she was distracted by the fact that Travis' lean brown fingers were close to hers as he continued to hold the foal gently yet firmly. Their eyes met, and she smiled spontaneously. She saw the dark pupils contract as his eyes widened and his gaze became intent. For a moment, Joanna forgot the foal, Sally, and everything else. Then she blinked and turned back to the filly.

"Er—what will you name her, Travis?"

Travis released the foal and it scampered back to its mother. "Brownie, I guess," he said rather absently.

"*Brownie?* But that doesn't fit her at all!"

"What are you talking about?" Sally put in, getting up to join them at the barrier. "She's brown, just like Belle."

"Brownie doesn't suit her personality," Joanna protested. "She should be called something sweet, like . . . Candy. Yes, Candy would be perfect."

"Imagine calling a ranch horse Candy," Sally derided.

"Why not?" Joanna persisted.

Leaving the horse box, Travis fastened the gate and cut the argument short. "Since Cassie won't be around long enough to call the filly anything, we'll stick with Brownie." He reached for the brim of his Stetson and settled it even lower on his brow. "Sally, you rode over here to give me a hand rounding up those steers in the south field, didn't you? Let's get on with it before Barney gets back from town with the new fencing." His cool glance at Joanna and a certain hardness to his jawline made it clear the thaw had been only temporary.

Immediately Sally's plain face was transformed. She threw Joanna a triumphant look as she left the barn with Travis, chatting happily with him about the prospective day's work.

Joanna walked to the barn door to watch them mount horses and ride away. Sally would make a perfect ranch wife someday, she thought sourly, suppressing an upsurge of feeling—it couldn't be jealousy, surely?—as her gaze followed the bright pink shirt. She, Joanna, wouldn't choose rounding up steers as the best way to forward a romance with a man. No, she'd prefer something more civilized. Sitting at a candlelit table, enjoying good food and conversation while the man-woman electricity generated and began to spark. . . . Travis would look handsome across that table, she thought. If he could learn how to smile, he might even be devastating.

A whinny from Belle brought her back to earth. As

Travis had said, she wouldn't be around long. This wasn't her world, and she'd better not forget it. With a sigh and a final hand-kiss to Candy, Joanna went back to the house.

On Friday night, she served supper with a strange feeling of restlessness, wondering whether she should follow through on her plan to offer her services a while longer. As usual, the conversation between Travis and Barney consisted mostly of laconic references to ranch matters. Up until now, she hadn't cared to initiate much conversation herself, thinking she might get into trouble by revealing too much of the real Joanna. But after a week of "pass the salt" and "more coffee?" she was ready to risk it.

Tonight, however, was to be different. Barney cleared his throat awkwardly as soon as he had finished his plateful of roast beef, buttered vegetables, and corn bread. "Cassie, that sure was a fine meal."

"Thank you, Barney." Joanna looked at him with some surprise. It was the first time either of the men had commented about the food. "I made a cherry pie for dessert, if you're ready for it."

Barney waited till she had cut and served him a large wedge of pie still warm from the oven and running with the thickened juice of tart red cherries. Then he cleared his throat again, causing Travis to look at him as well.

"Should have said something before, Cassie, about all the work you've been doing. Travis and me ain't been used to a woman doing things for us, not since Sarah died." He spoke gruffly, raising his eyes from the pie to look directly at her. "Sarah was Travis' ma," he clarified.

"That's okay, Barney," Joanna responded, smiling at him. "It's been a good experience for me. I never had the chance to run a big house before."

"So how do you like it?" Travis spoke in cool tones, his eyes narrowed and unreadable as he accepted the piece of pie she handed him. Wearing black corduroy pants and a gray open-necked shirt that was faded and soft from many washings, he looked relaxed yet charged with something she couldn't quite put a name to. He lifted a forkful of cherries and piecrust to his mouth. As his lips closed over the morsel, his glance held hers, waiting for her response to his question.

Joanna dragged her thoughts back to order. "Well enough," she said offhandedly. "In fact, since you seem so busy outside, I was wondering if you'd want me to keep on doing it for a while longer. I could use the wages."

Travis' face showed neither approval nor disapproval of the suggestion. Barney rubbed his bristly jaw with one callused hand. "Might be a good idea, Trav," he commented. "I ain't looking forward to my own cooking much. Kind of nice, the way Cassie's fixed up things around the house."

They all looked around, observing the changes. The table around which they were sitting was now placed in front of the bay window. Joanna had long since relegated the jar of battered knives and forks to the utility cupboard. The square table was laid with a linen tablecloth and good china and silverware, found in the recesses of a big sideboard in the living room. With the floors polished and the bare windows sparkling clean, the room was distinctly more pleasant.

"The place doesn't look too bad," Travis said grudgingly. "And the food is good and hot. I suppose we could work something out for a while longer. How much do you need?"

Joanna shrugged. If that was as close as Travis was going to come to saying she'd done a good job, that was his problem. "What's the going rate for domestics now?" she asked. "I only know about a secretary's wages. I'll need enough to pay for some clothes and to support myself until I can earn a first paycheck."

Travis pounced on this first hint of her background. "You were a secretary in Denver? Where did you work?"

Joanna broke off a piece of corn bread and popped it into her mouth. Chewing slowly, she regarded Travis warily. Finally she swallowed and said, "Here and there. I worked for a temporary agency for a time."

That was true. At least until the day she'd walked into Gerald's office and had been offered a permanent position as his secretary.

"Quite a comedown for you, scrubbing floors and doing laundry and the like," Travis suggested, his glance traveling down to her hands where they rested on the table by her plate.

Deliberately she spread out her fingers. Her fingernails were now cut short and were innocent of polish. A burn mark showed brownly across the back of her hand where she had caught it on the side of the oven. The corners of her mouth deepened as Joanna repressed a smile. When was he going to quit trying to get a rise out of her?

"Hardly," she said. "How do you think I got the money to pay for my secretarial course? I've worked as a waitress in hash-joints, too, and for a while I walked dogs for a dog-sitting service. Contrary to what you seem to think, Travis, doing housework doesn't push my nose out of joint."

Dark eyebrows lifted and Travis' eyes dropped mockingly to her neatly modeled nose. "I have to admit, it looks okay at the moment."

Barney's glance went from one to the other, fascinated by their reactions to each other.

"Besides," Joanna went on, determined to give Travis a taste of criticism for a change, "you've got a nice house, but it's plain to see the barn gets better attention. There's not a curtain in the house, and it's not very well arranged. Some of that furniture in the living room could be used better in here, like that big sideboard. It should be handy to the dining area, for storage. What you really need is a wife, not a housekeeper, Travis."

"*That* job isn't open, Cassandra," Travis said, startling her with his vehemence. "The house suits us just fine the way it is, doesn't it, Barney?"

Barney shook his head. "We had some roof trouble a couple of winters ago, Cassie, and we moved everything out of the way while we did the repairs. Stuff just never got moved back again afterward. Sarah used to have it fixed up real nice."

"If you'd help me with the heavy things, I'd be glad to fix it back again," Joanna offered. "Just as part of the *housekeeper's* job," she added with a lift of her chin at Travis.

"Don't get carried away," Travis said shortly. "Just the routine work will be enough. You don't have to get fancy. Do you want your money weekly or when you leave?"

Joanna experienced a sensation of relief. She rose and busied herself gathering up the used dishes. "When I leave will be fine. I assure you, I'll earn every bit of what you pay me."

"That you will," she thought he muttered as he threw his napkin down on the table and pushed back his chair. "Barney, how about a game of chess tonight?"

The next morning, Barney agreed to continue digging postholes for the new fence in the south field while Travis went into town for groceries and supplies.

"We stock up about once a month," Travis explained to Joanna as she was standing at the kitchen sink washing the breakfast dishes. "Are you sure you don't want to go in for anything?"

"No, thank you." She rinsed a plate and placed it in the drainer. "I'll spend the time clearing and rearranging the shelves to take the new stores. Unless you prefer that I do the shopping for the groceries." She hoped he wouldn't. An isolated ranch felt much safer than town, right now— less chance for the kind of notice she could do without.

"Probably save time if I do it, unless your vast work experience includes buying food in quantity as well as knowing how to cater to male appetites?"

Joanna gave him a bland look and turned back to the sink. "No, I never was in the army. You do the buying, Travis, and I'll stick to catering. Okay?" She looked at him brightly, her eyes very blue.

He didn't answer; a complicated expression swept over his somber features. With an irritated murmur that might have been a good-bye, then again, might not, he reached for the Stetson hanging by the door and shoved it down over his eyes as he left the kitchen. Joanna's hands remained motionless in the soapy water until the sound of the truck's motor died away in the distance.

Long before Travis was due to return, Joanna got restless. She decided to wash her hair, using Travis' shampoo. The crisp herbal scent of it pleased her and she worked it in lavishly. Towel-drying and finger combing the dark mass resulted in a gypsy fall of curls all about her face and shoulders. After a glance at the clock, she changed into a fresh pair of jeans and a T-shirt with a colorful sunset printed across the front. Instead of putting on her tennis shoes again, she decided to go barefoot.

The polished floors felt cool on the soles of her feet. She went the long way around to the kitchen wing, intending to check the storeroom again. The storeroom was part of a utility core handy to the kitchen. It had narrow shelves from floor to ceiling, bins for root vegetables and staples, and a large freezer. One could lay in supplies for a siege, she thought. Or, in this high country, for days of being snowbound in winter. She fell into a daydream wherein she fixed tasty meals from bountiful supplies for a grateful Travis while the snows piled up outside; long cozy evenings when they would . . .

With an angry shake of her head, Joanna pulled herself up short. What was the matter with her? She was city-bred, not cut out for this kind of life at all.

She heard the truck pull up outside the kitchen entrance. Hurrying to open the screen door, she had to step aside as Travis strode in carrying a fully loaded cardboard box.

The next few minutes were busy as boxes and bags were brought in and stacked, some on the floor of the storeroom, others on the counter in the kitchen. Joanna was amazed at the quantity Travis thought necessary for a month's supply of food for three people. Here was enough for that snowbound winter she'd been thinking of.

Aside from a quick glance at her as he entered, Travis was back to his usual, silent self. Joanna wondered why she had been so anxious for him to get back. She finished emptying the contents of one box onto the counter, then turned and bumped into Travis as he placed another box on the floor behind her. Startled, she grabbed at him to steady herself, and their eyes met and struck sparks at close range. His hands on her arms steadied her.

"Sorry. That was clumsy of me," she said breathlessly, vitally aware of the solid contours of his chest under her fingertips.

"It's a bit crowded in here," he acknowledged. "I got a few extra things." Slowly he released her, his hands sliding down her arms, creating a tingling sensation that didn't go away.

"We won't go hungry, that's for sure." Joanna tore her gaze from his and glanced at the box he had set down, a whole case of canned chili. "I had no idea you liked chili so much."

"It's okay. We keep it on hand for when we don't feel like cooking." He paused with his hand on the open screen door. "You're not expected to cook seven days a week, you know. The chili's for when you want a break."

"Wonderful stuff, chili," she answered, with a flashing smile. Secretly she felt jubilant. In a roundabout way, he had just acknowledged that she had earned her time off.

He smiled back, and Joanna almost dropped a carton of eggs. She stared after him as he went out the door. How was it possible for a man's face to change so much simply because he smiled naturally, with no trace of mockery? Was the thaw on again?

In a moment he returned with a fifty-pound sack of potatoes on his shoulder. "I'll put this away for you."

She followed him into the storeroom, watching him as he rested the potatoes on the side of a large bin. With a deft twist, he opened the sack, and the potatoes rumbled into the bin. He folded the empty bag and tossed it onto the nearest shelf.

Leaning against the side of the doorway, Joanna observed, "I haven't seen that many potatoes at one time since I was twelve and living with a family with five other kids."

This time he didn't pounce. "Not your own family, I take it?" Bending over, he reached into a box and chose an apple. Strong white teeth bit into the red fruit as he kept his keen gaze on her.

Joanna watched him take another bite of the crunchy apple. He crossed one booted foot over the other as he leaned back against the potato bin. Perspiration marked his shirt and gleamed faintly on the skin that showed beneath his partially unbuttoned shirt. He had worn the black cords again for his trip into town. The way they hugged his slim hips and long legs distracted Joanna.

"No. My father died when I was eleven, and my mother a year before that. I was raised by foster parents mostly."

"Sad story. Kind of a Cinderella, hmm?" His eyes wandered down to her bare feet. The plight of her early years didn't seem to move him much.

Joanna resisted the impulse to curl her toes as his gaze lingered. She spoke lightly. "Not quite. At least Cinders had a stepmother and stepsisters. The kids I was raised with were in the same boat I was. It's different, knowing the people who are taking care of you are doing it for the money. There may be some who do it for love—I just never met any of them."

"It doesn't seem to have damaged your psyche much."
He flicked a finger in the direction of the little golden sun
printed on her T-shirt. "Is that a sunrise or a sunset?"

"It depends whether I put it on in the morning or the
evening," she replied, tipping her head back to look at him.

"Cheerful little sun, isn't he?" The design was a piece of
whimsy; the sun-face had a painted smile that beamed with
friendly abandon. "Downright cheeky, I'd say." His expression told her he was alluding to more than her T-shirt.

"Some days I feel that way," she said. "And other days I
just think positive."

"The other day in the barn you were wearing one with a
rainbow on it." He regarded her quizzically. "I've heard
some people can put a whole philosophy on the back of a
T-shirt."

He discarded the half-eaten apple and reached out a hand
to grasp her shoulder, turning her around so he could see
her back. He drawled, "I get the picture on the front. I just
wanted to see if there was any more to the message." He let
her go, which was a good thing, because Joanna found his
touch far too disturbing.

He continued: "So you like happy suns and rainbows that
lead to pots of gold, do you? Is that the message? I didn't
think you were the type to believe in fairy tales."

"Oh, I don't know," she retorted without thinking. "I
bet some rainbows are worth checking out."

He stiffened abruptly. Like doors and windows slamming, she saw his guard go up.

"The only pot of gold around here, Cassie, is the one on
your T-shirt. You can forget anything else. Arne left
nothing except a few debts. He gave everything else away,
as you should know. Like I told you, this ranch is mine and
mine alone."

Why did this man always think the worst of her! Anger
made her forget she was supposed to be Cassie. She
laughed and tossed her head back.

"I've known men who could buy and sell a ranch like

this ten times over, Travis. If I wanted an easy life I could have had it without trying to con it out of a backwoods rancher.''

His lip curled in the expression she hated. ''And that's why you're here, dead broke? Pull the other one, lady!'' His eyes ran contemptuously over her shapely figure. ''You're a dishy-looking female, all right. But I'm not so hard up that I'd take what you've got to offer, at any price.'' He started to brush past her out of the storeroom.

''It's not on offer to you, at any rate,'' Joanna snapped. ''I'll wait till I get back to civilization, thank you!''

She could feel the heat emanating from his body as he stopped in mid-stride. The doorway became a constrictive space that was far too small for them both. Tension coiled in the pit of her stomach.

With a mirthless grin, Travis reached down and captured her wrist, pulling it upward between them. Her fingers were balled into a tight knot. ''This fist shows you're not so civilized yourself, *lady!*'' he said scornfully. ''But you're smart not to try and use it. I don't let women hit me . . . not even dainty little city women like you!''

He was very close. Joanna opened her fingers above the grip he had on her wrist and just managed to flick them against his cheek. ''Oh, no?'' she mocked.

Fire flashed in his gray eyes. He let go of her wrist, but only to grasp her body just above her waist; she could feel every one of his ten fingers as they dug in.

''A challenge, is it?'' he rasped, before his head came down and his hard mouth covered hers in anger.

They fought a silent duel, Travis seeking to dominate and subdue, Joanna to resist and rebel. His superior strength subdued her struggles, but could not prevent her sharp teeth from fastening on his lip. With a muffled oath, he lifted his head and glared down at her.

Joanna glared back.

''You started this, you know,'' he declared furiously. ''Why do you have to be so damned provocative?''

"Me provocative!" Joanna exclaimed indignantly. Her eyes fell on his lip and she saw that it was slightly swollen. That sobered her somewhat. Maybe she was partly to blame, but—"Let go of me, Travis. I'm not about to discuss who's to blame while you're holding me like an angry grizzly bear."

He tightened his grip. "You stay right where you are. It's safer."

Safe? The way her pulse was racing? His belt buckle was pressing into her stomach, and she could feel the male length of him against her thighs. A peculiar feeling of weightlessness came over her. Letting her head fall back, she looked up and saw an expression in his gray eyes that made her forget what she had been going to say. Blinking rapidly, she tried to gather her thoughts. Her voice was slightly husky when she finally managed to speak.

"How about if I apologize for being provocative? Then you could apologize for coming on too strong, and we could break this off." Another vigorous wriggle to free herself from his firm hold brought no results. At least, not the results she was striving for. "This is not a good idea," she said apprehensively.

"You're right." Like hers, his voice came out husky. His eyes were fixed on her mouth as though mesmerized. "It's not a good idea at all . . ." he muttered under his breath. His head lowered once more.

His mouth was moist and sweet on hers and tasted of summer and tangy apples. Joanna's lips parted involuntarily; she forgot all about resisting. Her fingers uncurled, stretched, and found the bunched muscles of his back through his sweat-dampened shirt. The heady male scent of him filled her nostrils.

Travis' grasp loosened and his hands moved over her body compulsively, as though he were unable to stop himself now that he had her in his arms. Long hard fingers, callused from rough work, trembled slightly as they caressed her breasts and the compact curves of her hips. The tight jeans she was wearing were no barrier, nor was the lightweight fabric of her top; her breasts seemed to fill his palms, peaking revealingly, responsively, as she leaned into his touch.

Deep inside, Joanna began to shake. She was keenly aware of his arousal, and the knowledge increased her excitement alarmingly. Without realizing it, she twined one bare foot around his corduroy-clad leg as his tightening arms lifted her into closer intimacy.

A smothered sound escaped his throat and his mouth broke away from hers. Then she was sliding down, her bare feet on the scarred leather of his boots before they touched the cool floor. His hands clamped on her arms and pulled them from around his waist. He thrust her away and she reached behind to steady herself on the door frame. They were both breathing in short bursts.

Travis looked at her with burning eyes. "If you kissed Arne like that, it's no wonder he did anything you wanted him to," he said through lips that barely moved.

"*I* kissed . . . Look here, Travis," she stammered.

"You're well named, Cassie, just like your namesake at the fall of Troy. I knew you'd be trouble the first time I heard of you."

"No kidding," Joanna murmured sarcastically. "Tell me more about how this was all my fault."

Travis hooked his thumbs in his belt and looked down his nose at her. The flush high on his sharp cheekbones was fading, but his eyes still burned. "You're a beautiful and sexy woman. Even when you don't open your mouth, you put out a challenge most men would find hard to pass by—so I'm not going to apologize. But I can do without the kind of trouble you represent, *Cassandra*. This won't happen again—believe me!" He started to turn away.

Smarting from the emphasis he put on the last words, Joanna put her hand on his arm to prevent his leaving. She gave him a warning of her own: "Don't read too much into a name, Travis. You might be making a mistake."

His gaze flickered over her once more, lingering on the softness of her mouth and flushed cheeks. Then he looked directly into her indignant eyes.

"I'd be a fool not to be on my guard against the kind of spell you put out, lady," he said. He looked pointedly at her hand and she dropped it as if his arm were hot. "I'll print it on a T-shirt if I have to."

"Don't worry, I've got the message. Now, how about getting out of here so I can get some work done?"

He seared her with one more look before he left, his boot heels hitting down hard with each angry stride.

Her eyes fell on the box of apples and she almost kicked it, only remembering just in time that she was barefoot. "Oh, blast!" she exclaimed instead. "I'm getting awfully tired of fighting your battles for you, Cassie Carlyle!"

Chapter Four

By the time Joanna had finished putting away the supplies, her temper had cooled, but her body was still agitated. She decided a walk might help her get things back in perspective. Angling away from the ranch house, she climbed a fence and crossed a field that brought her to a stand of scrubby pine trees. A patch of grass, dried to a pale straw color, looked inviting and she threw herself down. She leaned back on her arms, closed her eyes, and raised her face to the sun.

Why was she so upset? Before she met Travis, she had prided herself on her ability to keep her head when a man kissed her. So why did Travis spark her off like a Roman candle? She didn't even like the man!

Gradually the sun's warmth relaxed her nerves and muscles. Joanna opened her eyes and leaned forward, hugging her knees, smiling. Who was she trying to kid? Dislike Travis? What about that kiss? She shivered, remembering the way her body had responded to his touch. Good thing he was so determined to be on guard from now on.

Otherwise she might find herself in the middle of an affair she didn't want any more than he did.

She hugged her knees harder. No matter what he said, Travis *was* attracted to her. It restored her somewhat battered self-esteem to know he had been as strongly affected as she by what had happened in the storeroom. Maybe it was just that he had been alone too long, but somehow she didn't think so. In any case, now *she* was on her guard, and she wouldn't get caught like that again. Feeling better, she rose to her feet and continued her walk. By the time she returned to the house she was humming a country-western tune under her breath, her spirits quite recovered.

At supper that evening, Joanna felt Travis' gaze fix on her frequently, as if he wondered why she was so cheerful. She engaged Barney in sprightly conversation, not deliberately excluding Travis, but not waiting for his responses, either. His moodiness and abstraction increased. When she served the coffee, he absentmindedly creamed it twice.

"Do you play pinochle, Barney, or gin rummy?" she asked, not wanting to be left on her own again.

"Would you like a game, Cassie? How about you, Trav—feel like some pinochle? We can play three-handed."

Travis pushed his chair away from the table and stood up. "Some other time, maybe. Tonight I've got to bring those government forms up to date."

The sound of their voices as they played cards in the living room must have reached Travis in his room, but he didn't come out until late in the evening. He leaned silently against the fireplace wall, watching as Joanna triumphantly laid down her cards on the low table in front of the couch.

"Gin!"

"This female knows her cards, Trav," Barney exclaimed, chagrined. "She's beat the socks off me tonight." He stood and yawned sleepily. "Reckon I'll head for my bunk. Sure enjoyed the games, Cassie. 'Night, Trav." He nodded at them both, then left.

"Barney is such a kind man," Joanna remarked impulsively as she gathered up the cards, conscious that Travis was watching her closely. "Who is he, Travis? I can see he's more than just a man who works for you."

Travis moved in front of the fireplace and picked up the poker to prod the almost burnt-up logs into a bed of smoldering coals.

"I find it hard to believe Arne didn't tell you about him."

Joanna heard the antagonism in his voice as he mentioned Arne. Her buoyant spirits took a dive. "I was just asking." She felt his eyes on her as she stared at the smoldering coals. The moment stretched out, and her mouth drooped pensively.

Travis spoke abruptly. "Barney helped my mother finish raising us when Dad died fifteen years ago. When Mom died, he saw to it that Arne and I stayed in school; he knew that was what our dad had planned for us. Arne studied at the state university, and I went on to agriculture college."

Joanna stirred, and Travis' voice took on a harder note, as though to prevent her commenting.

"I don't suppose you have any idea what it meant to us, do you? Arne and I were the last of the Carlyles. Barney wasn't related to us, had no advantage to gain, but he cared enough to see two kids through a rough time. We could have run wild, but we didn't, because of him. He was someone to come home to—someone who really cared."

"I understand," Joanna said huskily.

"I doubt that you do, Cassie. That kind of caring has to come from inside; it can't be faked, and it can't be bought." Suddenly he clamped his teeth together and thrust his hand into the pocket of his jeans, "It's getting late," he said curtly.

Joanna blinked at him. He might as well have ordered her off to bed! And after implying she wasn't capable of honest caring, too . . . no, she had to remember he didn't really mean her, he meant Cassie. Uncurling from her position on the couch, she stood up. She'd better go on to bed, otherwise she might say something she'd regret. There was no way she could win.

She stopped at the door to the bedroom wing and glanced back. In the dim light she could see that his fist was still jammed in his pocket. His back was eloquently stiff, and he looked so terribly alone she forgot her resentment. That kind of aloneness she understood.

The following morning was Sunday. After taking care of the essential chores, Travis and Barney spent a good part of the afternoon with their heads under the hood of the pickup, diagnosing and curing a carburetor ailment.

Joanna wandered out to the barn to say hello to Candy, then went back into the house and got three cold beers. She carried them out to the big garage where the truck was kept.

"Anyone for a cold drink?" she asked.

A muffled grunt from Barney sounded approving. Travis straightened up and reached for an oil-streaked rag. He wiped some of the grease off his hands and arms, then took a can of beer and snapped the tab open.

"Thanks," he said. His eyes ran down the length of her before he lifted the can to his lips and drank deeply. Then he looked at her again with a frown of disapproval.

A high stool was handy, and after checking it for dirt or grease, she climbed up and sat down. Let Travis frown —she wasn't going to hide her shape just because he had a hang-up about her being provocative. Besides, in a T-shirt, there wasn't any way to hide. She was female and that was that.

"Are you planning to drink that?" he asked dryly.

"Oh! Yes, of course." She smiled sweetly and pulled the tab. Like him, she tilted her head back and took a long drink. When she lowered the can, a bit of froth clung to her upper lip and she licked her lips to capture it.

Travis crunched the can he held in his hand, then swore as the remaining liquid gushed out. He tossed the can into a trash bin and wiped his hand with the rag. "Barney, aren't you finished with that yet?" he asked in a goaded tone.

"I think I got it, Trav. There . . . that's it. Try 'er now."

Travis sprang into the cab and in a moment the motor reverberated deafeningly in the confined space. Joanna put her fingers in her ears. After a moment, Barney signaled and the sound died away.

"Sounds good, Trav," Barney said.

"Maybe. Let's take her for a spin and check it out on the road."

Barney took the can of beer Joanna was holding out to him and grinned his thanks. "How about coming along for the ride, Cassie?"

"No!"

Joanna and Barney stared at Travis.

"Uh . . . we'll just be out a short while, and there's grease all over the inside of the cab," Travis explained. "Come on, Barney, let's get it over with. You don't mind being on your own, do you?" The last was addressed to Joanna, the words dragged out with an effort.

"No, not at all," she lied. "I'll go in and start dinner." She slipped off her perch and started for the door.

Travis called after her. "Don't cook for me. I'll be out this evening."

She waved and went on to the house. As she crossed the veranda a dark frown creased her brow. So he was going out, was he? No doubt he had a date, like that other night when he had stayed out so late. Who was the woman? she wondered, gritting her teeth. Then she shrugged. Why was she getting all bothered about it? It was no business of hers whom he dated. She slammed the screen door behind her as she went inside.

She'd call Donovan again—that would take her mind off matters that didn't concern her. She needed to get in touch with the old man and figure out some way of getting those oil leases returned to him. Then she could start making plans for her own life again.

Her hand on the telephone, Joanna chewed thoughtfully on her lower lip. It was Sunday. Frequently Donovan spent Sunday with Kate Wilding, the widow of one of his partners from early days. He had taken Joanna with him once.

Joanna grinned at the memory of that afternoon. Kate was good fun and a marvelous cook. But Ellie, the niece who lived with Kate, had been a trial. She seemed to suspect that Joanna and Donovan were going to con her aunt out of her meager widow's pension or steal the silver off the table. Donovan made matters worse by keeping up a long-standing flirtation with the jolly-tempered widow.

Fortunately it was Kate who answered the phone.

"So you do understand, Mrs. Wilding? I'll leave my phone number for you to give Donovan, but please don't give it to anyone else. And to him only if he's alone. Would you mind doing that for me?"

"I expect him over today, Joanna. He should be here any time now," Kate said. "I'd be happy to give him your number. Ellie, hand me that pencil." There was the sound of a querulous voice in the background, and then Kate came back on the line. "What was that number, now?"

Joanna repeated Travis' number and thanked her, promising to stay near the telephone until Donovan called. She made a pot of tea and sat down to wait. She was on her third cup when the phone rang; she snatched up the receiver.

"Hello?"

"Joanna, honey, is that you?"

"Hi, Donovan." Joanna grinned into the phone. "Sunday dinner, huh? I figured you might be at Kate's."

He chuckled. "You figured right. I've been wondering when I'd hear from you. Are you okay?"

"Just fine. Listen, I want to get these papers back to you somehow. But Gerald will be on you like a duck on a June bug if we're not careful. Have you got any ideas?"

"Just a second, honey. Kate, do you suppose you and Ellie could start dishing up the dinner or something? I'll be there in a minute." After a moment, he continued in a lower voice: "I figure I can get a pal to get me a post office box without Lasker finding out. Then I can let you know what the number is. You gonna be staying put for a while?"

"For a while. But not too much longer, so do your best, will you? I think it'll work, but how are you going to pick up the papers once they get there?"

"I'll work that out when the time comes, don't you worry. I went to see a lawyer yesterday, and he said to just get them options back, and he'll take it from there."

"Fantastic. There's just one thing. When you call here, ask for Cassie if someone else answers the phone." About to explain further, Joanna heard the sound of the pickup truck returning. "I've got to go, Donovan. Don't forget. Ask for Cassie."

"Cassie, huh? You're going under a phony name, are you?" He chuckled again. "Okay, Joanna, I'll call soon as I can."

By the time Travis and Barney entered the kitchen, Joanna was busy preparing a roast to go into the oven. Both men looked satisfied with the results of their test run.

"I think I'll get cleaned up and go on over to the Temples' now," Travis said to Barney after a quick look at Joanna. "John wants me to take a look at that new bull, and Sally has some questions about Ag College."

Barney glanced at Joanna, then back at Travis reprovingly. "What about Cassie? It's not right to leave her on her own all the time."

"I doubt Cassie would enjoy herself over there. And I already promised to go." His glance at Joanna was a challenge. "But it's up to her. How about it, Cassie? Would you like to come?"

Joanna shuddered at the thought of going into that hostile household uninvited; at the same time she was pleased to learn Travis was not going to be spending an intimate evening with another woman. "No, thanks, I'd rather stay here," she said. "Are you going out, too, Barney?"

"Nope. There's a couple TV shows I like to watch Sunday nights." The older man seemed bothered. "Tell you what, Cassie, maybe we can shift some of that furniture for you now. We never have time during the week. Trav, if you'll give me a hand with the big sideboard before you go, I can manage the rest. Would you like that, Cassie?"

Barney seemed anxious to please her, and Joanna's heart warmed toward him. "I'd like that just fine, Barney, if it's not too much trouble. It sure would be a lot more convenient, since the china and the linens are stored there."

Travis surprised Joanna by not objecting. He gave her an oblique look and said as he started toward the door, "I'll be back to help as soon as I've showered and changed."

Later, when the massive sideboard had been maneuvered through the doorway and set in place across from the bay window, Barney approved the change.

"That's where your ma had that piece, ain't it, Trav?" He wiped his forehead with a large handkerchief. "The sideboard was here against this wall, and your ma's rocker was over there in the corner with that little table she used for her books and things. That flowery chair was on the other side. Kinda made a little talking spot." He beamed happily at Joanna and Travis. "I've got the table out at my place now, but I could bring it back."

"Don't bother, Barney," Joanna said.

"It's no bother," he insisted. "I like seeing things the way they used to be. I remember Sarah rocking away, reading and sewing in the evenings. Trav, remember how she kept her eye on you kids to see you got all your homework done, right there at the big table?"

Barney grinned happily at Joanna without waiting for Travis' response. He hurried to the door. "I'll just nip over to my place and get the table. Back in a jiffy."

They had removed the drawers from the sideboard while it was being moved, and now Joanna began replacing them. Travis silently helped. Intensely conscious of the scent of his freshly shaven skin and of his hair, still damp from the shower, Joanna fumbled with the silverware drawer, almost spilling its contents.

Her gaze kept going to him in spite of herself. She watched him lift a wide drawer heavily laden with linen. The muscles in his arms tensed, taking the strain easily. Her truant thoughts flashed back to those heated moments in the storeroom, remembering how those arms had felt when they were holding her—when he . . .

Travis turned his head and caught her staring at him. Flustered, she sought for a distraction. "What's this, Travis?" she asked, picking up a thick hand-bound book lying in a drawer along with a miscellany of catalogs and folders.

"That looks like my mother's old recipe book." He turned back to the drawer he was struggling to fit into its slot.

Thumbing through the volume, Joanna's interest was genuinely caught. "It doesn't look like any cookbook I ever saw," she said doubtfully. "It looks more like a diary. No, here's a recipe. My, what old-fashioned terms. This one calls for a fist-sized lump of fat, to be worked in well with castor sugar. I wonder whose fist, and what castor sugar is?"

"That's probably one of my grandmothers's recipes. Maybe even *her* mother's. Everything in there has been handed down over the years." Travis pushed the drawer in with a thump and turned to take the book from Joanna's hand. "This all used to be loose in a shoebox, then Mother made it into a book."

Travis held the book in his hands, and one callused thumb caressed the cover. A cheerful chintz fabric had been glued to the cardboard front and back, and the name "Carlyle" was hand-lettered on the front.

The screen door banged open and Barney came in, carrying a compact cherry wood table that had a drawer and several shelves built in below the square top. "Needs a little polish, Cassie,'' Barney apologized. ''Trav and I have let things go these last few years. Didn't seem much point, but now you're here . . .'' His voice died away and he looked uncertainly at Travis. ''Well, here it is, anyway.''

He set the table down with a flourish, then hurried to bring in a rocking chair from one of the unused bedrooms. Setting the rocker beside the table, he stood back and declared, ''Looks natural, don't it, Trav? Sit down there, Cassie, and let's see how it fits.''

Joanna hesitated, glancing involuntarily at Travis. With a harsh laugh Travis gestured for her to do as Barney had suggested.

''Go ahead, Cassie. Do you think the chair of a mountain wife and mother would fit you?''

Their eyes locked, and once again they were silently dueling. Joanna went over to the utility closet and took out the can of polish and her polishing cloth. She came back and knelt beside the rocker.

''Nobody's sitting in this until it gets some polish on it. It's a crime the way you two have let this lovely old furniture dry out!'' Defiantly she began to rub. ''Now don't you have anything better to do than stand around watching me work?''

For some time after they had left, Joanna continued polishing the high-backed rocker, feeling a strange longing to reach out and touch the woman who had sat in it, who had used the table for her books and small things. Who was still remembered by a weather-beaten ranch hand and a tall silent son. She sat on the floor beside the gleaming rocker and rested her forehead on the armrest. Only for a moment did she yield to the ache that could still catch her off guard, these many years since her mother's death. It did no good wishing for things you couldn't have.

Once she had put the house in order, it didn't take much effort to keep it that way, and Joanna had time to satisfy her curiosity about ranch life. She refused to let it bother her that Travis wasn't pleased by her interest. He rarely relaxed his guard when she was near, and she took a perverse kind of enjoyment in following him around while he did the routine chores in the barn and corral.

"Why don't you let me feed and water the horses, Travis?" she asked early one morning when she was watching him distribute hay and feed. "I'd like to, really I would."

The pungent, earthy smells of the barn surrounded them. Travis emptied a bucket of oats into a feeder and looked at her skeptically.

Joanna became conscious of her appearance, aware that he was critically scrutinizing her jeans, which had been torn and now bore a neat patch over one knee. The jeans were so old they were incredibly soft and fit her like a second skin. Her top today was one that proclaimed the wearer was going to "Keep On Truckin'," but it had seen better days as well.

"Don't you ever wear a dress?" Travis asked unexpectedly.

Joanna blinked at him. She thrust her hands in her pockets and shrugged. "I'd look pretty silly wearing my party dress while I'm working around the ranch," she replied. "That's the only dress I have with me."

Travis set the bucket down with a clang against the wall. "Well, why don't you get something else the next time someone goes into town? You're earning enough to pay for it." He sounded irritated.

"Since when have you become an arbiter of fashion around here? What difference does it make to you what I wear?"

He looked exasperated and walked to the corral where Sam, the big bay he usually rode, was hitched to the rail. "If you don't know, I'm not going to tell you," he said shortly. But the way his eyes were drawn to the tight fit of her jeans gave her a pretty good idea what was bothering him.

She concealed a smile. So he wanted to start covering her up, did he? Knowing she was playing with fire, she came closer as he tightened the girth and prepared to mount.

"You didn't answer. How about me taking care of feeding and watering the horses? I know how; I've been watching you."

Whatever Travis would have said in reply was lost in a hissing, squalling noise from the barn. The next moment Spats and Curly erupted from the barn in a ball of fur and nails and teeth. Oblivious of their surroundings, the cats carried their battle into Sam's territory, causing him to sidestep nervously. Travis, caught in midair just before he could swing his leg over the saddle, swore as he tried to maintain his balance.

Joanna darted in to save the cats from Sam's stamping hooves. She realized it was recklessly foolish the instant she made her move, but it was too late. Sam plunged backward to avoid woman and cats, and Travis fell sideways, his foot caught in the stirrup. He grunted heavily as he struck his back against the corral rail, then dropped the rest of the way to the ground. When Sam stopped backing, Travis freed his foot, but not before his ankle had taken a twisting wrench. Grimacing, he dragged himself to his feet. Joanna rushed to help him, her heart beating fast in her throat.

"Travis, let me . . ."

He pushed her aside and clung to the rail, catching his breath. "What were you trying to do, you idiot?" he gritted. "Everything would have been fine if you hadn't ducked under Sam's head that way."

"You shouldn't be standing up," she protested, ignoring his rebuke. "That was an awful crack you took across your back—you might have damaged your spine."

His glance was cutting. "No thanks to you if I didn't, but I think I can make it to the house if you and those cats stay out of my way. You'd better wrap those reins around the rail."

Sam submitted docilely as Joanna tied him up once more. Curly and Spats were nowhere to be seen. She slipped under Travis' arm and took a firm grip around his waist.

"Come on," she said. "I'm a lot stronger than I look. Go ahead and lean on me."

His body was warm where it touched hers. Wrapping his arm around her neck and catching hold of his wrist, Joanna managed to keep from staggering as she took part of his weight, and they began the slow walk back to the house. They were both short of breath by the time they reached the veranda steps. Travis grunted every third step and Joanna worried about the damage he might be causing by his stubborn determination not to give in. When he let go of her and reached for the veranda rail to pull himself up the steps, she couldn't contain her anxiety.

"Talk about idiots, Travis Carlyle!" she scolded. "You could be making it worse, walking all this way when you don't know how badly you're hurt. Won't you please lie down and let me call a doctor?"

"And stay on the veranda for the four hours it'd take Doc Andrews to get here? I'd rather make it to my bed." He reached the top of the steps and stood teetering for a moment. "I wouldn't mind a hand again, though," he said, and Joanna knew it had cost him something to admit it.

Maneuvering awkwardly through doorways, they finally arrived in his room, and he carefully sat on the edge of the four-poster bed. Joanna spared a thought for the beautiful patchwork quilt as he lowered his fully clad body onto the bed.

"Let me take off your boots, Travis. No . . . maybe we'd better wait for the doctor. What's his number?"

"Don't bother," he gasped, his face white. "I just bruised some muscles and twisted my ankle."

"Travis . . ." she began to object.

"Don't argue, Cassie. I've fallen off more horses than

you have, and I know what I'm talking about. Once I get in a hot tub, I can soak out the worst of it. If you want to help, give me a hand with these boots. Slowly, please."

Joanna saw he was determined and stopped protesting. She set her mouth grimly and reached for one of the scarred boots. Although she pulled as gently as she could, she saw the sweat break out on his forehead before the boots were finally off. The breath she was holding rushed out along with Travis' gusty sigh of relief.

"Thanks," he said tightly, his eyes closed. "I think I'll rest a bit before I try to get to the tub."

"Isn't there something else I could do for you?"

"Why all the sudden concern for my well-being? It's somewhat out of character for you, isn't it?"

Joanna reminded herself for the hundredth time that she could hardly blame him for thinking the worst when she couldn't counter his charges with the truth. "Maybe I'm a reformed character now, Travis. Wasn't that what you had in mind for me when you agreed to let me stay on and work at the ranch?"

He looked at her again and a muscle jumped in his hard jaw. "I'm not sure what I had in mind. I know one thing—there's something about you that doesn't fit. I get the feeling you're hiding something."

She didn't blink an eye under his scrutiny. "And you assume it's something bad, of course."

"I'll find out what it is before you leave here, you can be sure of that."

Joanna felt a warning thrill. She laughed and gave him a provocative look from under half-lowered lashes. "I prefer to think of you as a reformer, Travis. Who knows, you may save me yet from my wicked ways."

"You admit to the wicked ways?"

"One can always make improvements. I'm willing to pick up a point or two along the way." She saw a spasm of pain cross his face, and she stopped her sparring, saying crisply, "Look, you're hurting, Travis. Why don't we drop this discussion of my character and see about getting you into that bath? Are you going to let me help or not?"

"I can manage to undress myself," he said shortly. "But you can run the bath for me if you will."

She regarded him doubtfully, then shrugged and left him. After filling the tub, she wondered whether he would snap her head off if she offered to help him to the bathroom. Undecided, she lingered, listening for the sound of movement from his bedroom. The minutes passed, and anxiety began plucking at her insides. There was nothing but silence from the room down the hall.

Chapter Five

She hurried down the hall. Whether he thought he needed help or not, she just couldn't walk away and leave him. At the doorway she paused. Travis was lying between the sheets with the quilt tossed to the foot of the bed; his jeans and his shirt were crumpled on the floor. Beads of perspiration marked his brow, and he had turned white again. He didn't look like he was going to make it to the bath.

She went hunting in the bathroom closet and found a heating pad and some aspirin. Returning to Travis, she plugged in the pad and silently stood over him till he opened his eyes and looked up at her. He must have seen the determination in the set of her jaw, for he gave her a crooked smile and allowed her to slip the heating pad in place behind him while he downed the aspirin.

She helped him ease back on the pillows, extremely conscious that the concealment offered by a cotton sheet was little different from no covering at all. Had she thought he was too thin? Her senses were telegraphing a different impression now. Though pared of all extra fat, his body was that of an athlete; his muscles were smoothly firm, sculptured across his chest and down his torso to his narrow hips. Under the sheet his thighs were strong and masculine.

Inhaling sharply, she turned away. Good heavens, what was the matter with her? It was ridiculous, the power he had over her senses! She seized on an excuse to put some distance between them. "Barney won't be back until this afternoon, Travis. I think I should unsaddle Sam."

He may have replied, but she was already moving and didn't wait to hear. Her breathing didn't return to normal until she reached the corral. Sam stood patiently while she fumbled with the straps and buckles and then heaved the saddle and back pads off. She let him into the corral and was shutting the gate after him when the sound of an approaching vehicle announced a visitor.

The battered Chevrolet sedan looked familiar. As it came to a halt in the driveway outside the kitchen veranda, Joanna recognized the smiling figure at the wheel. It was Maggie Puldowski, the farmer's wife she had met the day of the funeral.

"Good morning," Joanna said as she approached the car.

"'Morning, Cassie," came the booming response. "Thought I'd pop over and see how you're doing. Heard you were still here." The snapping black eyes surveyed her with sharpening interest. "You look hot and bothered, girl. You got some kind of problem?"

Joanna explained in a few words and Maggie clucked in sympathy.

"Flat on his back, is he? I'd better take a look at him." She climbed out of the car, and they went into the house through the kitchen entrance.

She was quick to note the new arrangement of the furniture. "You've fixed things in here real nice, Cassie." Her approving glance took in the bowl of yellow marguerite daisies on the table.

Joanna smiled, pleased. She had found the flowers only that morning growing among the vegetables in Barney's garden. The daisies gave the family room a cheerful touch it had lacked before. On an impulse, she picked up the bowl and took it with them to Travis' room.

"How do you and Travis get along?" Maggie asked.

"Just fine." Joanna grinned suddenly, thinking about the rocky road their "getting along" was following.

Maggie's black eyes twinkled. "Now, why do I get the idea that there's a lot more to that 'just fine' than meets the ear?"

When they entered Travis' bedroom, he raised his hand from his eyes. "Did you have any trouble unsaddling . . ." He broke off when he saw who was with Joanna. "Maggie!"

"Hello, lad. What's this I hear about you letting an old nag like Sam throw you?" The older woman's tone was affectionately teasing as she came over to the bed and smiled down at him.

"Is that what Cassie told you?" Travis looked over at Joanna, watching her as she arranged the bowl of flowers on top of his dresser.

"I told Maggie you were showing me how *not* to get on a horse," Joanna gibed. Then she queried, "Don't you think we should call the doctor, Maggie? He landed awfully hard on that rail."

After questioning Travis closely, Maggie seemed to be satisfied he had correctly diagnosed his condition. "Could be worse," she said finally. "Main thing is to stay flat for a while and get some wet heat on those back muscles. Cassie, you see to it he doesn't get off this bed except to go to the bathroom."

"Now, look, Maggie . . ."

"Hush, boy. Cassie won't mind keeping an eye on you." The stout little woman reached for the quilt at the foot of the bed. "What's Sarah's heirloom quilt doing thrown down here?"

She held the quilt up so Joanna could see the intricate pattern. Though the tones were muted with age, the quilt contained a multitude of prints and colors; the tiny quilting stitches were a marvel of workmanship as well as being an important element of the design.

"That's the flying geese pattern, Cassie. See the triangles like wings? Those little pieces were cut from old dresses, shirts, and any spare scrap of cloth that came handy. Nice piece of work, isn't it?"

Joanna picked up a corner of the quilt appreciatively. "It certainly is, Maggie. It's a work of art."

"Art is right." Maggie sniffed, folding the quilt carefully. "There's a wedding ring quilt in that chest over there that belongs in a museum, but Travis won't give it up. What do you mean by putting this one on your bed like an ordinary blanket?" She shot her last question at the man in the bed, bringing the conversation back to its original course.

"Quit lecturing, Maggie," Travis returned. "Can't you see I'm in no condition to defend myself?" He sounded aggrieved but the corners of his mouth were twitching.

"In that case, you'll hold still while we fix you up with something wet and hot for your back. That dry heat's not going to do you much good. Cassie, you can make a cold pack for his ankle."

"You make me sound like a canning project," her patient grumbled.

Maggie chortled. "Now you mention it, maybe I should mix some vinegar in the hot water. That's an old home remedy that helps sometimes."

"It's sour pickles you put up in vinegar, isn't it?" Joanna asked, catching on. "I don't think we've got enough vinegar on hand for Travis."

Another ten minutes saw Travis settled to Maggie's satisfaction. He looked ruffled, and his humor was a little the worse for wear.

"See here, Trav, don't mess with that pack now it's in

place. You ought to have a warm bath to keep those muscles from tightening up, but I guess you'll have to wait for Barney to get you in and out of the tub. I doubt you'd let Cassie and me help you there."

Travis' grim expression endorsed Maggie's statement.

"Wouldn't you like a cup of tea, Maggie?" Joanna asked, coming to his rescue. "How about you, Travis? I've heard sweet tea is good for shock."

"You have, have you?" he replied ominously. "Well, I've had about enough home treatment for one day. Lay off, won't you, Maggie? I've had all the poking and prodding I can stand. I've had everything except peace. And privacy," he added pointedly.

Maggie chuckled, not at all offended. Giving him a pat on the cheek, she motioned to Joanna to precede her out of the room. "Just you be good, Trav, you hear? And don't give this girl a hard time while you fret yourself into a temper because you're stuck in bed."

"I'm not going to be stuck long, you can be sure of that," he muttered as they left the room.

Joanna put the kettle on, and the tea was soon brewed. She enjoyed the next half hour; Maggie was a mine of information about the local community and had a good grasp of the history of the area.

"Ezekiel Carlyle, now, Travis' great-granddad." Maggie waved her tea cup enthusiastically. "He was a real ripsnorter. The old boy left off prospecting for silver to settle down and homestead this place when Minna, his wife, came west to see what was keeping him away from Boston so long. She was a match for him, by all accounts. That's their bed, in Travis' room."

"The four-poster? I've been wondering about that. It seems awfully large for an antique. I thought older beds were a lot smaller, more like our three-quarter-sized beds."

Maggie nodded. "Ezekiel was a big man, way over six foot. He had a wood-carver make that bed to fit. Though I heard Minna used to complain it wasn't big enough!" A hearty chuckle shook her plump cheeks. "Must not have been. They had five strapping sons."

"What happened to the family, Maggie? Travis said he was the last of the Carlyles here." Joanna refilled their cups with hot fragrant tea.

"A couple of Ezekiel's boys went on to California and were lost track of. And the sons and grandsons that didn't get killed in the First World War got killed in the second. Travis' dad made it through Korea, but there wasn't much left of the Carlyles by then."

"So Brad and Sarah decided to adopt Arne," Joanna observed pensively.

Maggie snorted. "Decided? Not exactly. Arne got dumped on the Carlyles like a cat that's taken out in the country and left to survive as best it can."

Joanna felt an inward shock. "Didn't Arne have any people of his own?" she asked. "Who was it that . . . dumped him, as you said?"

"Arne's folks were some kind of cousins of Sarah's. Flighty people. They came by and asked if they could leave him while they took care of some business in the city. Brad said yes, of course. They felt sorry for the boy. Arne was an undernourished little kid, smaller than Travis, who was a year younger. The Carlyles thought they'd feed him up, then talk to the cousins pretty hard when they came back for him."

"But the cousins never came back," Joanna put in, foreseeing the end of the story.

"Never did. The boys got on real well; Travis stood up for Arne whenever the other kids gave him a rough time like kids do with outsiders. Sarah used to say it was Arne who'd get into trouble, but it was Travis who'd come home with the black eye."

Joanna smiled at this picture of the valiant young Travis. "Yet Arne went to the city instead of staying on the ranch with Travis," she mused aloud.

Maggie nodded. "The ranch never meant to Arne what it

did to Travis. That's why the folks fixed it so Arne had enough money to get along on, and left the ranch to Travis. But you probably know all about that.''

"Well, I . . . that is, I . . .'' Joanna stammered. She had been so interested in the unfolding of the story she had forgotten her own supposed connection with Arne.

"Don't worry.'' Maggie's eyes were keen as she smiled kindly. "I'm not going to pry. How you and Arne came to get married is no business of mine. When he told George and me about it, he only said you would be coming when the time was right, and that we should be good to you for his sake. It's too bad . . .'' She hesitated, then caught Joanna completely off guard. "You wouldn't be pregnant, would you?''

"Pregnant?'' she repeated stupidly, then felt heat rise into her cheeks. She answered flatly, "No, I'm not.''

"Now, don't mind me asking you that, dear,'' Maggie hastened to say, her own cheeks a little pink. "It's just that I know Arne didn't have anything to leave a wife, unless . . . well, never mind. I'd have been happy if you were pregnant, Cassie. This house needs children in it again. And speaking of children . . .'' She set down her cup and got to her feet briskly. "My daughter's bringing her family over for supper tonight, and I'd better get on home and start fixing it. Thanks for the tea, dear.''

Joanna was relieved to wave good-bye to her visitor. All that friendly interest could be unnerving when you had something to hide. She went back into the house to prepare soup and a sandwich for Travis' lunch.

He was lying propped up on his pillows staring out the window when she came in with the tray. The hot pack was a heap of wet towels and plastic wrapping on the floor, and she picked them up and put them aside after setting the tray on his lap.

"Can you manage the soup, or shall I feed you?'' she asked with a straight face and a gleam in her eyes.

"Now, don't you start, '' he growled.

Joanna leaned against the rolltop desk and her mouth went in at the corners mischievously. "Maggie's known you a long time, hasn't she?"

Travis responded with a reluctant grin. "When a woman has known you since you were in diapers, and changed them for you, too, you don't exactly tell her where to go when she treats you like you were still six months old." He picked up the spoon from the tray. "But that doesn't mean I'll take it from anyone else."

Joanna smiled. "I like Maggie. She and Barney are the kind of people that make a difference in the world. Just like Arne . . ." She stopped abruptly. She had almost said "Just like Arne must have been." Avoiding Travis' suddenly alert gaze, she walked over to the cedar chest at the foot of the bed and ran her hand over the folded quilt Maggie had placed on top.

"Tell me about this quilt, Travis," she said. "Do you know which one of your people made it?"

"My great-grandmother. Like Arne, you were about to say?" He returned to her previous comment, ignoring her diversion.

A bit of gray ribbed sateen drew Joanna's attention, and she ran her finger over the fine line of stitching that held it in place. "I only meant . . . well, Arne was a good man, wasn't he?"

Travis didn't reply, and at last she had to look up at him. His eyes were fixed on her intently, but there was no trace of the bitterness he had shown before when the subject of Arne had come up.

"Is there more to the story than I figured, Cassie? Arne always said I was too hasty—that I jumped to conclusions too quick sometimes." A slight smile warmed his gray eyes. "You have to admit you haven't given me much to go on—I've never seen a woman who could clam up the way you do. You don't volunteer much, do you? Earlier, I accused you of hiding something—but it could be that I just haven't asked you the right questions. Will you answer if I ask them now?''

Joanna caught her lower lip between her teeth and hesitated. Should she tell him now, or not? He sounded reasonable at the moment, but she didn't trust his explosive temper. He thought that all she had to explain was the reason why she hadn't come sooner—as Cassie. When he heard just how far he had been led down the garden path . . . No, her instincts told her to keep her mouth shut. A man in pain wan't really ready for bad news, no matter how reasonable he sounded. She'd do better to go on as she was for a while longer.

He was looking at her, his eyes expectant. Mustering her resolve, while feeling like a heel for ignoring his overture, she said evasively, ''Let it go, Travis. It's better not to rake over old coals. It wouldn't serve any purpose. Any explanation I gave you would probably sound like a lie or an excuse to you, anyway, so—better just let it rest.''

The expectant gleam faded, replaced by a fleeting look of—disappointment? Then his face took on its closed look, shutting her out. Upset, and not at all sure she hadn't made a bad mistake, she edged toward the door.

''Don't bother running away.'' The weariness in his voice stopped her. ''Right now I don't have the energy to fight with you about it. I'm not very hungry. Would you mind taking this tray with you?''

Joanna returned to take the tray; she added the discarded towels, then stopped in the open doorway to look at him again. The sheet had fallen down around his waist, and he was looking away from her, out the window.

Her eyes lingered on the faint sheen of his skin, half hidden where the hair on his chest grew thickest. A rush of feeling swept over her, and appetites she had laughed at in others took possession of her imagination. She hungered to explore him with her hands, with her mouth and tongue, to revel in the warmth and maleness of him. She wanted to find out if the curling hairs were soft and silky, or whether they were crisp and wiry. In a sudden full-blown fantasy, she tasted the saltiness of his skin, traced a line slowly up to the vulnerable part of his throat just where his shirt collar protected it from the elements, leaving just that little bit as soft as a woman's skin. . . .

"Cassie!" Travis' voice was hoarse, almost strangled. "Stop it!" A dull flush had risen to his cheeks. His eyes had gone dark and there was a tiny licking flame in their depths.

"I . . ." His voice snapped her back to reality. Dear heaven, what had he seen in her face? He must think—"I'd better take these things back to the kitchen," she gasped, and fled the room.

When Barney came in later, he took over Travis' care, for which Joanna was thankful. She no longer trusted herself where her reactions were concerned—not with Travis Carlyle, at any rate! Accustomed to feelings of mild attraction, occasionally, to men who met her, wanted her, and pursued her—Joanna had never felt attracted in such a physical way to any man before. It disturbed her, made her feel oddly restless. That evening Barney took the chess board into Travis' room.

"It'll cheer him up. He hates to be sick, or stuck in bed when he's not sick." He stopped for a moment in the doorway. "Sure you don't mind being on your own, Cassie? You can come, too, if you want. We could play cards instead of chess."

"No, I'll be fine in here, Barney," she said hastily. "I can watch television or read—you go ahead."

About nine o'clock she couldn't stand it any longer. It struck her that she really should take the men some refreshments—some coffee, or maybe some lemonade. At least she should ask them. The floor was cool under her bare feet as she went down the hallway. Travis' door was slightly ajar; as she was about to tap on it, she realized they were talking about her and her hand was arrested in midair.

"I don't think that's a good idea, Trav," Barney was

saying. "Cassie'll tell us herself, before long. She's been closemouthed so far, but that could be because we set her back up that first week, being so unfriendly and suspicious."

"You know what we thought about her, Barney, and why we thought it. Arne . . ."

"You know as well as I do that she's not that kind of woman. I could see it after the first couple of days. I reckon we judged her before we heard her side. She's too proud to clear things up until she proves some other way how wrong we were." Joanna heard a gravelly chuckle. "Proved she could work as hard as any two other women, didn't she? That's a spunky gal, Trav. Stubborn, too. You be nice to her for a change, and she'll open up, you'll see."

Travis growled an answer, but Joanna fled without hearing it. Safely curled up in her corner of the living room couch, she pondered over what she had heard. Barney had put his own interpretation on her silence and was trying to persuade Travis to see it the same way. Would he succeed? If Travis insisted on his answers—there wasn't any real excuse for not giving them to him, was there? The question struck an uneasy chord, and she decided not to think about that until she had to.

She was leafing through the cookbook-diary that had belonged to Travis' mother when Barney came in just before ten o'clock. He coughed to get her attention.

"Cassie?" He waited till she looked up and then asked awkwardly, "Do you suppose you could give Travis another of those hot packs? He needs it to relax those muscles so he can get to sleep."

"Why . . . why, I suppose . . ." Caught off guard, she stumbled over her words. "I'd rather you . . ."

"Thanks, Cassie. I've got some things I need to do at my place. I left the towels and things in the bathroom. See you at breakfast!"

He scurried out, and Joanna wondered what he was up to. He had helped Travis into a warm bath earlier, fetched and carried his supper tray. Why was he so busy with other things now?

Putting the book aside, Joanna made her way to the bathroom. She ran the water till it was as hot as she could stand, and soaked a large folded towel. After wringing out most of the water, she quickly placed the towel in a sheet of plastic and then on another dry towel. She then carried the simple pack into Travis' bedroom.

He looked at her in surprise when she entered. He was propped up on double pillows.

"Where's Barney?" he asked, his brows drawing together.

"He had things to do," she replied lightly, forcing herself to meet his look with outward calm. "He asked me to fix this. Here, will you lean forward just a bit so I can get it behind you?"

She reached under him to place the dry towel so it would protect the pillows. And all the while she felt his eyes scorching her face. The clean scent of his skin rose to assault her senses. Of necessity her hands touched his back and the firm sleekness of him sent a wayward shiver down her spine.

When she raised her lashes to look at him, the smoldering heat of his gaze almost undid her.

She straightened abruptly, her hand falling away from his shoulder. "You should take some more aspirin, Travis. Otherwise you'll have a hard time sleeping tonight." Her voice came out huskily, sounding as though she were being deliberately seductive, but it was too late to clear her throat and start again.

He stared up at her. A flush crept up his cheeks, and his lips twisted. "You're doing it on purpose, aren't you?"

"I don't know what you mean," she said, bluffing.

"Those seductive looks you're giving me—the flowers—all this touching. You fixed it with Barney for him not to come back, didn't you? And now you're doing the Florence Nightingale bit. Or is it the Theda Bara bit?"

Now she knew he didn't subscribe to Barney's theory about her. He was just as suspicious as ever. Her temper began heating up. She hadn't meant anything by looking at him—at least, not what he thought. If he started throwing insults around . . .

"You're after something," he accused, his eyes narrow and hard. "Barney says I'm wrong about you. He's quite a fan of yours, but I'm sure you know that. It's a good thing I'm disabled. It might be my only defense against your brand of seduction."

"Why, you egotistical . . ." Joanna was all the more incensed because she knew it was just the other way around. It was he who was affecting her, and all she could do was try to convince him they were both mistaken. "How many times do I have to tell you you've got nothing I want?"

His lip curled. "Then just drop all this phony 'nurse' act. Whatever you're trying to accomplish, you're wasting your time."

Joanna's face burned at his jeering tone. She picked up the hot pack and balanced it in her hands. "So I'm wasting my time, am I? Travis, I think your mind is stiffer than your back, so . . ."

His raised hand couldn't prevent the steaming package from landing on his head; she pivoted sharply on her heel to escape, but his other arm snaked out and encircled her hips. Twisting around, she saw the flare of temper in his eyes as he pulled the wet towel from his face and flung it aside.

"You short-tailed bobcat!" His hand clamped around her wrist, effectively holding her in a position leaning over the edge of the bed. "You'll be sorry you did that!"

"Careful!" she gasped. "You'll hurt your back again."

"Never mind my back," he grated between clenched teeth. "What did you gain by that dumb fool trick?"

Her fingers were busy trying to loosen his grasp, but he wouldn't let go. "Nothing. I lost my head," she answered sharply. "You asked for it, you aggravating man!"

He tugged and she fell half across him, causing him to

grunt with pain. She froze, afraid of hurting him. Angrily she cried, "What do you think you're doing?"

A strange look of confusion altered his furious glare, then his eyes darkened with purpose. "I believe I'm losing my head," he groaned thickly. "And you know it, you witch. . . ." Letting go of her wrist to reach up and bring her head down to his, he melded their mouths together in a searing contact that turned Joanna's bones to water.

The next few moments proved that even a disabled man was a force to be reckoned with in his own bed. Sprawled on top of Travis' almost naked body, with only a flimsy sheet between them, Joanna was plunged into a maelstrom of sensation that surpassed any sensual fantasy she had ever heard about. Without changing his position an inch, Travis brought her quivering body into line with his, and his hands stroked her in ways that sent her blood pressure skyrocketing. He wooed her with his mouth, his lips and tongue drawing responses from her she hadn't dreamed it was possible to feel. She should have been objecting, but she couldn't. Her head was floating somewhere in space, and her body was being melted and turned into liquid that formed just as he wanted it. And as she wanted it, too.

Her hands slid under his shoulders, her fingers curling up around them to caress his smooth naked skin. Her breasts, crushed against his chest, felt full and hard; she ached to touch him unencumbered. As though of the same mind, he suddenly tugged her top free of her jeans; another pull and she felt her bra come undone. Air touched her skin briefly, and then there was nothing at all between her bare breasts and the hard contours of his chest. The curling hair on his body was both crisp and silky against her skin, and she moved, enhancing the prickling sensation.

A low growling sound came from his throat; it was like the hungry purr of a big cat, confident the means of satisfying that hunger was within its grasp. The long incendiary kiss ended, and he buried his face in the softness of her throat, breathing heavily.

"Cassie—I want you so much," he groaned. The movement of his lips on the tender skin just below her ear caused her to shiver with raw pleasure. "You don't know what it's been doing to me, knowing you were just down the hall, wanting you in my bed till I've been almost crazy—"

Her heart lurched as she heard his admission. His words echoed the clamoring of her own senses. It's never been like this before, she thought hazily. I didn't know . . .

He groaned again, on a slightly different note, then laughed raggedly. "My back is killing me, I'm hurting all over, and I still can't keep my hands off you. Cassie . . ."

Cassie—this time the name reverberated in her head. No—something was wrong. Not Cassie—Joanna! Her brain suddenly connected with her body. What am I doing? she thought in anguished shame. I'm about to make love with a man who thinks I'm someone else! Someone he hates . . . No, it was impossible! She couldn't do it, couldn't let it happen. . . .

Revulsion rippled through her, enabling her to wrench away and sit up. With both hands, she pulled down her top, reaching back with shaking fingers to fasten her bra. When at last she looked at him, she saw her own conflicting emotions mirrored on his lean face as he realized she meant to withdraw. Arousal mixed with pain changed rapidly into angry frustration, then his mouth twisted in the beginnings of a wry grin.

"Not one of the smartest things I've done recently," he observed. "I thought I was hurting before. Now . . ."

Joanna hastily rose from the bed. With both hands she smoothed the hair he had turned into a wild tangle. "You do get physical, don't you?" she queried shakily, needing to anger him, regain the distance they'd had between them before.

"I could say the same for you," he retorted, cocking an eyebrow and letting his gaze wander down to her tautly defined breasts, still rising and falling faster than normal.

She sought for words to put things back on their former

footing. But could she? His words still rang loud and clear—he wanted her in his bed. And I certainly gave him reason to think I wanted it, too, she castigated herself. Oh, yes, I wanted it, or thought I did. . . .

She reined in her wayward thoughts. At least she could try to backtrack. Her heart was pounding sickeningly. In her emotional tumult, she was aware of a new fear—some fear she couldn't quite identify. Trying to push it down, she spoke aggressively:

"Look, I'm sorry I lost my temper and dumped the hot towel on you. Frankly, you make me lose my temper easier than anyone I've ever known. We agreed we wouldn't let this sort of thing happen again, didn't we? You were right—it complicates things too much. Just because we're alone in the house here, we can't . . . we can't . . ." Her voice trailed off.

"Can't we?" he asked harshly, but she was hard put to meet his gaze frankly, much less answer his question. "What would it complicate in your life, Cassie?" he asked. "Are you already tied up with some man? Was there someone else besides Arne?" His questioning gaze was neither jeering nor sardonic; it told her that the answer was important to him.

She felt a flutter of panic. Her hands were showing an alarming tendency to shake and she thrust them into the pockets of her jeans. "Travis, I don't see that's any of your business. I don't have to answer to you for my private life. I'm just passing through, after all."

"Just passing through," he repeated. His eyes took on the opaqueness that prevented her from guessing at his thoughts. "I suppose our corner of the world seems pretty confining to you, doesn't it?"

"I wouldn't exactly call your corner of the Rocky Mountains confining," she replied, trying to make a joke of it, but not succeeding very well. "I . . . I like it a lot more than I thought I would, as a matter of fact. But I'll be moving on pretty soon, so it doesn't really matter what I think.''

His brows were drawn together; he had raised an arm above his head and the corded muscles revealed to her that his control was only a surface thing. The temptation to go back and crawl into that big four-poster with him warred with her desire to run. The strength of the temptation shocked her and, stifling an exclamation, she did run—down the hall to her own room where she firmly closed the door.

Hours later she was still tossing restlessly on her pillow, frustrated and puzzled in equal measure. She had never before reacted so strongly to any man, never lost her head to the point of forgetting everything except how he made her feel in his arms.

She kicked the bed coverings from her perspiring body and stared upward at the darkened ceiling. So why should she care what name he called her, if it were just a biological need? She had reacted—reacted violently when he had called her Cassie, his wanting and his need plain in his voice. There was something else in his voice, too—something that called to her on a level she didn't want to explore. His lovemaking was dangerous!

If she wasn't careful, she might get trapped into thinking she was falling in love with him, and that was simply impossible. No, what she wanted—needed—was to be free, and stay free. Like her father, she intended to see much more of what life had to offer. Travis had been right when he said his corner of the world was too confining for her.

As for a casual affair under another woman's name, she couldn't indulge in that kind of thing—not with Travis. He had made a genuine overture toward her today, and she had ignored it. His show of anger toward her, his suspicion, hadn't she earned it? Then the way he had held her, kissed her—her instincts told her he was beginning to care in spite of his confused feelings about Arne and Cassie. It was one thing to carry on a masquerade so long as it didn't really hurt anyone, but in his bed—when he was hating himself for wanting her? No way! ·

As long as she kept in mind the fact that she was dangerously susceptible to Travis' potent brand of sensual masculinity and was reasonably cautious about their being alone together in this big house . . .

She rolled over and pounded her pillow. Things would *not* get out of hand. All she had to do was keep a grip on her traitorous senses long enough for Donovan to call. Then she could fly free and far, and Travis would become only a sweet, sensuous memory. She wouldn't even tell him who she was. She was much safer that way.

Chapter Six

Joanna was grilling bacon the next morning when the sound of a door opening caused her to look up. She saw Travis entering from the hall, dressed in jeans and a dark blue work shirt. He was carrying his boots in one hand. His expression dared her to say anything as he stiffly crossed the room and sat down at the table.

"Well, good morning," she said dryly. "I thought you were supposed to stay in bed for a couple of days."

"Do you suppose I could have a cup of coffee?" he asked sourly.

She brought the coffee pot and a cup and set them down in front of him. A faint grimace passed over his face as he reached for the pot, and she knew that for all his stoic front, he was suffering considerable discomfort.

"If you trained as a vet, and this is the way you treat yourself, I'm glad I'm not a horse under your care," she said half humorously.

His gaze wandered slowly over her face, taking the time to study her mouth, bare of lipstick, before it dropped to the happy sun logo on her T-shirt. His firm mouth curved slightly, mockingly, as though at a memory he found amusing. "You don't think I'd take good care of you?"

Joanna was enveloped in a sudden wave of heat. Any reply she might have made was forestalled by Barney's entrance. His eyes darted from Travis over to Joanna at the stove. There was an expectant look on his face.

"'Morning, Cassie," he said cheerfully. "'Morning, Trav. How d'you feel this morning? Reckon Cassie's hot pack fixed you up pretty good, hmm?"

Joanna glanced over at Travis as she took the sizzling bacon from the grill and laid the pieces on a folded paper towel. The glint in her eye warned him to watch his words.

He merely drawled, "She fixed me up so good, I'm ready to get back to work. You were going to take the truck out to the lower field today, weren't you?"

After a short protest, Barney gave in to Travis' firm insistence that there was nothing wrong with him. The ranch hand threw a disappointed look in Joanna's direction that puzzled her until she remembered him asking Travis to be nice to her so she would open up about her past. Apparently he thought all they needed was an opportunity to be together and Travis' niceness would show itself. She cracked an egg against the side of the skillet so forcefully that the sticky contents ended up in her fingers instead of in the hot fat in the pan.

After breakfast Barney helped Travis put on his boots. Joanna closed her ears to the muttered imprecations Travis loosed before the task was completed. They heard the sound of a horse being ridden up to the kitchen veranda. A moment later Sally Temple appeared at the screen door. She rushed inside without ceremony. Her gaze, full of concern, fastened on Travis, still sitting in his chair.

"Travis!" she exclaimed. "I came over as soon as I could. Maggie called last night and told us about your accident, but Mother wouldn't let me come over until this morning. Shouldn't you be in bed?"

"There's nothing wrong with me," Travis responded irritably. "There's no need for a fuss."

"But, Travis . . ."

"I appreciate your concern, Sally, but frankly, the last thing I need is another female fluttering around me. Why don't you just go on back home? I'm going out with Barney in the truck today."

Barney went outside, muttering something about driving around to the door. Travis rose painfully and limped toward the door. The telephone rang, and since he was nearest, he reached for the receiver.

"Hello!" he barked. His eyebrows went up and he turned to Joanna. "It's for you. A man."

Joanna gingerly took the receiver he was holding out to her. It had to be Donovan.

"Hello?" she inquired cautiously.

"Hello, honey." The old man sounded concerned. "Guess I picked a bad time to call, didn't I? Whoever that was, he didn't sound too happy."

"That's okay. I'm glad to hear from you." Her comment went with a cool expression for Travis' benefit; he was looking at her grimly, his lips tight and his brows drawn together.

"I'll make it short and sweet then."

He gave her a number, which she committed to memory; she hoped it would stick there until she could write it down. "Thanks, I have it," she said, choosing her words carefully. "I'll write soon. Please take care, won't you?"

"Don't you worry about me none. I guess I won't be seein' you for a while, so I just wanta say thanks, honey. I won't forget your part in all this. You be real careful, you hear? It's not gonna be safe till I get those papers to the lawyer."

"I understand." Joanna waited until she heard the click at the other end before she replaced the receiver on the hook. It was unfortunate that Donovan had such a loud penetrating voice.

Travis was looking at her closely, his eyes narrowed and opaque. "Keeping in touch with your friends in Denver, I see. Donovan, was it?"

Joanna started. How on earth did he know that? Then she remembered. He had heard her on the phone that other time, when she had called Donovan by name. "Yes." She saw no harm in admitting it.

"No doubt he—and your other friends—are missing you."

"No doubt," she said repressively. "Weren't you going out with Barney? He just brought the truck around."

He looked at her darkly, then reached for his Stetson and crammed it down on his forehead. He limped noticeably as he walked outside to the truck.

"It's all your fault, you know!" Sally burst out, and Joanna turned to look at her. "Travis shouldn't be walking around with an injury like that."

"He's a grown man, Sally. Neither one of us could make him do anything he didn't want to do. So how could it be my fault?"

"He had to leave the house because he wanted to get away from you!"

"Don't be silly," Joanna chided, knowing there was a strong possibility Sally was right.

"You think you're pretty smart, don't you, coming here and hanging around where you're not wanted. Maggie was bragging to Mother about what a wonderful job you've been doing here, how interested in everything you are. I just bet you are—you're interested in finding out what you can get out of Travis!"

"You've said enough, Sally. I know how you feel about Travis, but . . . ."

"You don't know how I feel! What do you know about anything? If you hadn't been here, Travis would have stayed home today and let me take care of him."

"If you put on a tantrum every time you don't get your way, I'm surprised he hasn't sent you packing before this."

Joanna was getting tired of Sally's childish display of temper and spoke more sharply than she intended.

Sally flushed to her hairline and her hands clenched into fists. "You're the one he ought to send packing—and he will, too! You fooled Arne somehow, but Travis is too smart for you. He's not going to be taken in by your flashy looks and la-di-da city ways! Not after Christine, and she was twice as pretty as you!"

"Christine?" Joanna queried blankly.

"His wife, of course." Sally's eyes narrowed suspiciously. "Everybody knows how she got him to marry her, then couldn't take it when he brought her here—she went back to the city faster than you could say scat to the cat! If you're after him, too, you might as well forget it. What use are you on a ranch? Why, you can't even ride a horse! *I've* been riding since I could walk!"

Joanna stared at Sally's angry face as though she had never seen her before. Travis . . . married? Well, why not? Strange that she should feel shocked, almost betrayed. . . .

With a triumphant sniff, Sally stalked past her. She yanked the screen door open, then turned and looked Joanna scornfully up and down. "If you want to know what I think, I think there's something phony about you. What proof have we got that you were really married to Arne? Just your word for it's strange you only showed up the day of his funeral.

"You have a vivid imagination, Sally." Joanna smiled with an effort, concealing her dismay.

Sally's eyes flashed resentfully. "I think Travis should check you out, that what I think. And I'm going to tell him so, too!" The screen door slammed behind her as she ran out and down the steps and mounted her horse. When she saw that Joanna had followed her to the door, she hurled a parting shot: "Why don't you just go on back to the city where you belong, like Christine did. Nobody wants you here!" With a flick of the reins, she urged her mount away at a gallop, leaving Joanna staring after her.

The girl's words rang in her ears, echoing her own inner doubts. Then Joanna pulled herself together and forced herself to think about getting rid of Donovan's papers. The rural postman would pick up the mail if she could find the postage. As the only likely place for stamps was Travis' desk, she overcame her reluctance to pry and went there to hunt through the drawers. As she looked, she couldn't help wondering if she would find a photo or snapshot of Travis' former wife. The stamps were in the first drawer she opened, however, and a guilty sense of wrongdoing prevented her from looking further. What possible difference could it make to her what Christine looked like?

Still arguing the question with herself, Joanna went to get the manila envelope from its hiding place in her bedroom. After a moment of blankness when she was afraid she had forgotten the address Donovan had given her, she thankfully recalled it and wrote it down. While she made the half-mile walk to the mailbox her mind turned the new information this way and that, as if it were a key she could use to unlock several puzzling doors.

An early unsuccessful marriage would explain why Travis was not married now. Also it could explain why Travis was so suspicious of the woman he thought to be Cassandra Carlyle. Cassie's treatment of Arne must seem even worse in view of his own experience. Could that be why Arne had been so reticent about Cassie? Because he had known of Travis' prejudice against women who might be anything like Christine?

Reaching the end of the long driveway, Joanna crammed the manila envelope into the mailbox and raised the metal flag to notify the postman there was mail to be picked up. What a relief to have those valuable papers off her hands at last! Donovan, in possession of the lease options once more and backed up by the law, would be a match for Gerald now. She was free to go on her way.

The sun was well up; the scents of pine and growing grasses were carried to her nostrils by a light breeze.

Raising her head, Joanna breathed in deeply and looked down the empty road. The prospect of starting off down that road seemed uninviting; a feeling akin to pain tightened her breast. Why wasn't she more excited about her newly gained freedom? It was what she wanted, wasn't it? After last night she was just asking for trouble if she stayed.

Turning back toward the house, she thrust her hands in her pockets and kicked at a loose stone, trying to make sense of her mixed-up emotions. Something peculiar seemed to have happened to her in these short weeks, and she still was not sure how she felt about it. Working in the homestead was different from anything she had known before. There was no sense of drudgery, or of being trapped. Instead as she had cooked and cleaned and polished she had felt a sense of continuity with the past, almost a kinship with the women who had lived here before. It was as though their love and caring remained to be carried on into the next generation; as though the emptiness of the house was a kind of expectancy, a waiting for the woman who would inherit that caring along with Travis.

Joanna laughed softly in self-mockery. If she started seeing herself in the role of Travis' wife, it was time to have her head examined. Even if she loved him, which she didn't, the very idea of his falling in love with someone who had entered his home with a false identity, a dubious background, and an inherited instinct for a nomad's life was ludicrous. The sooner she took off, the better. When Travis had recovered a little more from his injuries, she'd ask for her wages and quietly leave. "Cassie" would disappear without a trace—unless the real Cassie took it into her head to show up some day.

It was easier to make the decision than to carry it out, she found. One day went by, then another, then she stopped counting. There seemed to be no urgency to make the break and many reasons to stay on. The Colorado summer was pleasant, and each day there was time to explore the nearby fields and to enjoy the view from the smaller hills. If Sally made good on her threat to warn Travis, Joanna never heard about it. In fact, he treated her with a neutral kind of courtesy she had trouble getting used to. It was almost as though he were being careful not to frighten her off. Whatever it was, it made it possible for her to relax her guard a little.

On one of her explorations she came across Barney's cabin, tucked away in a stand of trees. Potted geraniums ornamented the front porch; it looked homey, and Joanna thought she could understand why Barney preferred to have a place of his own, rather than just a room in the big house.

She visited Candy and the other horses often. The filly was growing and changing almost daily, and Joanna loved to watch her prance around, showing off each new accomplishment. Travis was once more doing the barn chores, and Joanna insisted he take seriously her offer to feed and water the horses. Finally he agreed, after watching her demonstrate that she knew how to handle the routine.

"You've got the hang of it," he acknowledged. "Go ahead, if you're sure you want to, Cassie. You've gone a little horse crazy, haven't you?"

"I suppose so. I used to wonder what it would be like to have a pet. I never expected to have a whole barnful."

"They're not pets," Travis said with amused exasperation. "They're work animals."

"Oh, yeah? I saw you petting Belle in there and fussing over her. How about that?"

A slight flush appeared on his cheekbones. "Belle isn't coming along quite like she should. She takes a bit more attention, naturally."

"Naturally," Joanna agreed, her eyes sparkling. She just loved to see Travis caught out in a show of affection. "Just an old workhorse?"

"There's a piece of hay caught in your hair," he said, blatantly changing the subject. "Here, I'll get it out. Hold still."

He moved close and Joanna inhaled sharply. His fingers were deft, but the hay was well entangled in her fine hair.

"Ouch!" She winced as he pulled strands of her hair along with the straw.

"I told you to hold still. There—it's out." He smiled down at her—that spontaneous smile that had the power to interfere with her breathing. "You're as skittish as Candy. Just as pretty a mane, too." His hand returned to caress her hair lightly, as though he found its soft silkiness fascinating.

She sought to turn away the kindling warmth of his gaze with a flippant remark. "I'm glad you've conceded that Candy suits the filly a lot better than that awful name Brownie."

Travis gave the curl his finger was probing a sharp tug. "Did I say Candy?" he retorted. "I meant Brownie."

"No, you didn't mean Brownie. She wouldn't answer to anything but Candy, now, would you, sweetie?" Disturbed by his nearness more than she cared to admit, Joanna turned to the filly, who had run over to greet them.

"She'd be as likely to answer to 'sweetie' or 'darling,' since that's what you call her more than half the time."

Joanna looked up into his face as he smiled down at her with no trace of mockery, and her heart almost stopped. Emotion flared upward from her breast, and she had to forcibly stop herself from swaying toward him. The names he had spoken, mimicking the crooning note she used when talking to the filly, shook her to her core. In a moment of blazing realization, she knew that she wanted to hear him say those words to her, and only her. How long had she been lying to herself? She didn't just "like" him; she didn't just feel tremendously attracted to him—she was in love with him!

"Cassie?" His hands came up to take her by the arms. "Are you all right? You look pale all of a sudden."

"I . . . I'm fine," she answered dazedly. "I . . . excuse

me, I have to go up to the house." She tore free from his grasp and brushed past him out of the barn. Fortunately he let her go. Several minutes later she watched from the kitchen window, her thoughts in a turmoil, as he rode away from the corral.

She still hadn't come to terms with her discovery when, later that evening, Barney questioned her about her quietness as he was helping her with the supper dishes. Travis had gone to his room to take a phone call a few minutes earlier.

"Is anything wrong, Cassie? You've been awful quiet tonight. Have you and Trav had another fight?"

"I'm fine, thanks." She smiled at him but didn't reply to the second part of his question. If only it were as simple as a fight—she could handle that. Right now her instincts were shrieking that she'd better run as fast and as far as she could from an emotional tangle that had gotten completely out of hand. She had been an idiot to stay as long as she had.

"You know, Cassie," Barney observed as he waited to dry the plates she was rinsing and stacking in the drainer, "Arne didn't tell us much about you, but I figure he knew how well you'd fit in here, knew you'd bring some life back to the old place." He looked at her warmly and a little anxiously. "I'm glad you've stayed on."

Joanna looked at Barney with pain darkening her eyes. She would have liked him to know the truth. But if she couldn't bring herself to tell Travis, she could hardly tell Barney.

Barney misread her glum expression. "Don't hold it against Trav if he still seems kind of short with you at times, hmm, Cassie? It's hard for him to let down his guard."

He wasn't the only one, Joanna told herself. Impulsively she introduced the name of the woman who had been in her thoughts since Sally revealed her existence. "Barney, do you think I remind him of Christine?"

"Arne told you about her, hmm?"

"What happened, Barney?" Joanna felt compelled to ask.

Shrewd black eyes studied her for a moment, then, as though satisfied by what he saw in her face, he continued. "Two kids getting married too young, that's what happened. Christine was a nice girl, but she was town-bred and she didn't really know what she was letting herself in for. If she had come to stay at the ranch first, well, I suppose they might not have gotten married at all. They split up—Travis went back to finish school, and she went to Nevada for a divorce."

"And Travis?"

"Trav was pretty well cut up. Took him a while to get over it. But he's fine now." His last comment was accompanied by a smile that was meant to be reassuring.

Was he? Joanna doubted it. Why else had he been so hard on her from the first day? Not always hard, though, she amended, thinking of that afternoon in the barn. Then she stiffened her resolution. Staying in his orbit was just asking for trouble. And that was why she was leaving as soon as possible.

When Joanna went into the living room with Barney, Travis was already there. Pulled by a force she couldn't control, she watched him as he stacked wood on the fire he had just built. The dark pants and shirt he wore emphasized his long lean body. His proportions were perfect, she thought, admiring the breadth of his shoulders and the narrowness of his hips. He turned his head and their eyes caught and held.

"What did Maggie want, Trav?" Barney asked.

"George and Maggie are having a gathering at their place Saturday night. We're all invited."

Joanna drew a deep breath and decided that now was as good a time as any to tell them of her plans.

"I'm not sure I'll be here Saturday," she said, walking over to stand near the fire. Without looking at the man standing so close to her, she added, "I've been thinking it's time I was on my way. I was wondering if you or Barney could give me a lift into town Saturday morning."

Silence followed her quiet statement. Joanna winced as Travis dropped the iron poker into its holder with a metallic clatter.

Barney's jaw fell in dismay. "Aw, no, Cassie! I thought . . ."

With a tight smile, she turned to the older man. "Sorry, Barney. I hadn't planned to stay this long, actually. Travis is fine now, and you aren't nearly so pressed with the ranch work. I'm not really needed around here, so . . . well, I'd better move on."

Barney would have argued further, but Travis cut him off. He hadn't taken his eyes from her since she had made her announcement.

"Better not make a fuss, Barney. I expect Cassie has had enough of the high country. She obviously wants to get back to her friends and the life she's used to."

Joanna stifled an instinctive protest. What did it matter why he thought she was leaving? The important thing was to cut her ties here before it was too late; she was afraid she was going to leave a large chunk of her heart behind as it was.

"Well," she said, "what I'd really like to do now is play cards or something. How about it?"

His brow furrowed, Barney nodded. "Sure, Cassie, but . . ."

"I'm pretty good at poker. My father taught me, and he was an expert. Would you like to try a hand or two?"

"Get the cards and chips out, will you, Barney? We might as well see just how good she is."

The planes of Travis' face were stark. His glittering eyes were at odds with his cool, indifferent tone of voice. They weren't indifferent at all. He looked as if he disliked her intensely, and it was an effort for her to go on acting normally. "Let's play in here by the fire," he suggested. "Unless you'd rather use the table in the kitchen?"

"No, this is fine," she agreed, sitting on one end of the couch. Travis took the other end, and Barney drew his chair up to the coffee table, his face troubled.

Travis dealt the first hand, and the game began. An hour later Joanna's pile of chips had increased respectably, mostly at Barney's expense. While Travis took time out to replenish the fire, Barney complained with forced heartiness: "Trav, what do you think of this girl? When she opens those blue eyes, looking like butter wouldn't melt in her mouth, and then raises for all she's worth, I can't tell if she's got all aces or nothing but a low pair, can you?"

"You shouldn't fall for her bluffing, Barney," Travis replied, straightening up with no remaining trace of stiffness in his movements. "Maybe you're getting tired. You put in a long day today, didn't you?"

Barney looked at him with a puzzled frown for a moment, then his face cleared and he nodded vigorously in agreement. He rose to his feet, an elaborate yawn creasing his face. "You're right. It's been a long day, and I think I'll turn in. But you two keep on," he said hastily, when Joanna started to get up as well. "It's still early for you young folks. See you in the morning," he called out as he left the room.

Joanna picked up the loose cards, shuffling them deftly. The room felt suddenly too warm, and she wished Travis hadn't put that last log on the fire. His eyes were on her again, hooded and unrevealing. She waited for him to make some comment about her plans to leave, but instead he sat down again on the couch and reached over to cut the cards.

Another hour sped by. Joanna's pile of chips diminished as the stacks in front of Travis increased. He played to win with a single-mindedness he hadn't shown earlier. Distracted and a little bit jumpy, she made mistakes, then tried to compensate by playing strictly by the book.

"Raise you," Travis said, putting out two blue chips.

"I'll match that," she responded, her eyes as free of expression as she could make them. He smiled wolfishly and dealt the final cards of the hand.

The ten of hearts joined the king, queen, and jack of the same suit face up before her.

"Well, well," Travis murmured. "Could it be the lady has a flush? Maybe even a straight flush? Or maybe she's got nothing but a lot of nerve?"

"You know how to find out," she stated, pushing out a good half of her remaining chips.

"Hmm." He contemplated the pair of sixes showing in his own face-up hand, then pushed out the largest stack in his pile of chips. "It might be worth the price to see if you've stopped playing it safe."

Joanna lowered her eyes to her hole card, turned down in front of her. She'd have to bluff or throw in her hand. Pretending nonchalance, she pushed her entire pile into the pot and challenged him with a look. He slid another stack forward—he'd raised again, and she had no more chips to call.

"Worried about not having the stakes to back your winning hand? I can take your IOU, you know," he suggested with an arrogant air that set her teeth on edge.

"IOU for what? You know we're only playing for chips."

"Are we?" he answered coolly. "I thought we might play for something else."

"No," she said slowly, on her guard. "I don't have anything else I want to put up."

"Aren't you forgetting your wages? I still haven't paid you for the work you've been doing."

"No, thanks. I need that money for bus fare."

She was taken aback by the fierce expression that came over his face at her words.

"In that case I'll take some answers to a few questions," he said harshly.

"I don't like answering questions," Joanna said, her eyes clashing with his. "Especially not on demand."

"Afraid?" he taunted.

"I'm not afraid of you, if that's what you're asking," she replied, her face feeling warm and flushed.

Travis shoved the rest of his chips forward. "Then I'll take the IOU and call!"

Joanna tore her eyes from the challenge in his and reluctantly turned her hole card up, revealing the ten of clubs that spoiled her flush and left her with only a pair of tens. Her jaw clenched tightly when, with another wolfish grin, Travis flipped his fifth card over and revealed the six of hearts.

"Too bad about the flush," he mocked. "Looks like my three of a kind beats your pair. Now let's have the answers."

She stared at him, her thoughts disjointed and conflicting. Maybe she did owe it to him to answer his questions before she went. But not this minute, she pleaded with herself. Not when I'm so vulnerable to him. In the morning, perhaps— when she felt more able to handle his reaction. She'd tell him, and when she left Saturday he'd never know . . .

"Really, Travis, I think we've gone far enough with our game tonight," she said, pretending annoyance. "I'm tired. I think I'll turn in. We can talk some other time."

"I don't think so."

His hand on her shoulder stopped her from rising, and she subsided into her seat. She might have known he wouldn't let her get away with it.

He leaned toward her, and she could see the fine lines that radiated from the corners of his eyes. Under the high cheekbones two long indentations marked the sides of his mouth with tension. "You owe me, remember? Cash or answers. Which do I get?"

Joanna stared back at him, her eyes wide. How would he react if she stated baldly: My name is Joanna Randall, and I never heard of Arne or Cassie or you before that night in the bus station. I'm on the run from a crook who probably wouldn't hesitate to break both my arms to get back the papers I took from him. And I'm fathoms deep in love with you!

She couldn't think while he was so close. Unaccustomed tears sprang to her eyes. It was all so impossible.

His hand tightened on her shoulder, and he glared at her in frustration. "What is it that's making you look so shattered?" he ground out through his teeth. "Talk, damn you! I've tried to remind myself of what you did to Arne—tried to fit it in with the way you act, and look, and smile, and it doesn't work! You're so beautiful, Cassie. Beautiful and desirable. I know a woman can be one thing on the outside and something else underneath. But you . . . what are you? What were you to Arne?"

His eyes searched her face intently. "What kept you from coming with him when he came home to die?"

Unable to answer, Joanna closed her eyes to escape his burning eyes. With a muffled cry, he drew her into his arms.

"I can't help it—I have to hold you, touch you . . ."

She trembled as she felt his touch—on her lips, across the line of her jaw, down the pale skin of her throat. His lips were warm and dry as they brushed her mouth. When his fingers slipped under the neckline of her blouse and traced the upper swellings of her breasts, Joanna's heart began tripping at double rate and she could hardly breathe. Forces began to build deep inside—if he kissed her, she wouldn't be able to keep him from discovering her love. She tried to make herself pull away, but her limbs wouldn't obey. His voice came to her from far away, as if in a dream: "The thought of you married to Arne, sleeping with him, tears my guts out. When you said no, the other night, I promised myself I wouldn't touch you again, but I can't seem to think of anything else. . . . Look at me!"

Helplessly she opened her eyes and almost went under at the expression she saw on his face as his head came closer.

His lips claimed hers in a kiss that broke through the fragile restraints she had been keeping on her own need for him; her arms curved about his shoulders and her fingers twined fiercely in his hair. She cared for nothing except the fact that she was in his arms again at last.

His mouth was moist now, his probing tongue deliciously welcome. Unresisting she followed him down until they lay full length on the soft cushions of the couch. She was giddily aware of his intensely aroused state as he threw one leg urgently across hers. His hand trembled as it explored the length of her side, lingered on the curves and indentations of her body. His fingers touched her breast above her heart, his palm pressing delicately, then greedily, into her softness.

"Your heartbeat tells me this is doing the same thing to you that it's doing to me," he murmured thickly, trailing kisses on the tender skin around her ear. "You've wanted me, too, haven't you? I've seen the look in your eyes . . . show me, Cassie—touch me."

This time she didn't even register the name by which he called her; responding recklessly to his impassioned words, she slid her hand into the opening of his shirt, freeing buttons. Her palm curved on his muscled chest. Closing her eyes, she first felt the thudding of his heart under her spread hand. His nipples were tiny pebbles that stood out distinctly in the mat of curling body hair, and she lingered over them; then she let her sensitive fingertips trace the silky growth down over his midriff to his waist. She was intoxicated by his warmth and the slight dampness of his skin.

The breath he took sounded more like a groan, and he fumbled with the buttons of her blouse. His hand slipped inside her bra, claiming her soft fullness possessively.

A gasp escaped her throat and was swallowed as his mouth closed once more on her parted lips; the aching sweetness he was making her feel promised greater delights somewhere just beyond her reach, if she could just get closer . . . if he would just go on kissing her. . . .

His hand on the snap of her slacks caused her breath to stop in her throat. A memory flashed—that breathless moment at the top of the ski slope—she knew that in another minute she would be careening wildly down a suicidal slope, heading for disaster. For a moment, recklessly, she didn't care, then with sudden clarity she saw a sated Travis looking down at her in disgust. The contempt in his eyes—the hard, hating line of his lips—Liar! he would say— Cheat!

"No!" She wrenched her mouth from his and struggled to push away the weight that kept her body captive. "Please stop, Travis," she managed to cry out when he would have drawn her back into closeness. "I don't want this . . ." His reflexes were slow to respond, and she was able to struggle out of his arms. Sliding to the floor with a thump, she stared up at him while he gazed down at her in shock.

It was a moment before he moved. Then he sat up, his chest heaving as he tried to bring his breathing under control. She couldn't bear the look of confused frustration on his face, but fear was half suffocating her. I couldn't stand it, she thought wildly. It was bad before, but now I know I love him— If he turned on me later—hating me—

"No, don't, Travis," she cried out in an agony of distress and confusion when he started to reach for her again.

Chapter Seven

Scrambling to her feet, Joanna dusted her hands on her slacks. She lashed out at him in her need to put him off.

"You may have won that hand of poker, Travis, but it doesn't give you any rights over me! If you want to hold back my wages, then that's all right with me. I can always hitchhike out of here." She started toward the bedroom wing, but Travis was right behind her.

"Wait!"

She half turned her head, looking down at his hand on her arm, and it dropped away.

"Don't worry. I'm not going to insist on any rights, and I don't intend to keep your money. Just hear me out."

"I'm listening," she said with difficulty. Her throat was closing up, and she had to blink fiercely to keep the tears back. She felt frustrated, guilty, and yet angry, too. Mostly at herself for getting into such an indefensible position in the first place.

"Look, I came on strong because I didn't want you to talk about leaving."

Joanna swung around and confronted him with wide eyes. "You *want* me to stay?" she asked incredulously. "I thought you'd be cheering when you saw the last of the notorious Cassandra."

"You know that's not true. Not anymore. Didn't you hear what I said a few minutes ago?" He was uncomfortably close; close enough to start her heart hammering again.

"You must have heard what I said, too. It's time for me to be moving on." Her voice lacked conviction; she wanted him to convince her there was a chance for them.

"You can't go—not now!" His voice became fierce. "Do you think I haven't tried to fight this from that first day? I could have sent you away, but I didn't. Something about you stopped me. I decided I had to prove to myself that you were all the things I thought you were; that I was crazy to let a pair of blue eyes and a face that . . ."

He stopped, raking a hand through his already ruffled hair. Joanna had to look away. She started to button her blouse with shaking fingers, fumbling. With a resigned twist of his mouth, Travis brushed her hands aside and helped her, ignoring his own loosely hanging shirt.

"Cassie, if you're honest, you'll admit you've stayed on here for the same reason I couldn't let you go. A minute ago in my arms . . ."

"Don't! It's not that simple—"

"I think it is, but I can see you're scared of something. I won't push you. You don't trust me, yet. I'm trying to make up for the way I treated you when you first came. I didn't believe Arne when he said we had to go carefully with you, that you could be scared off, but I do now."

Joanna made a sudden movement, and he caught her by the shoulders. He said urgently, "Don't run away—stay, and I'll give you more time to get used to the idea. Hell, I'm only just getting used to it myself! But we've got to give it a chance!"

She was silent, unable to deny the singing excitement that beat through her veins.

"It's too much of a gamble . . ."

"You play a good hand of poker, Cassie. Don't back down now, not with the stakes we've got riding on this hand."

Joanna looked up at him. His smile was a little off center, but she could see the sincerity in his eyes. Her heart swelled with love for him, and against her better judgment, she capitulated.

"I hope I don't regret this as much as I regret that three of a kind in your last hand, Travis, but—I'll stay."

He grabbed her in a bear hug and swung her off her feet. "You won't regret it, honey—just relax and enjoy it!"

"Put me down! Travis, I said I'd stay, but only for us to get better acquainted!" She was flustered as he let her slide to the floor again. "Promise me, Travis, you won't confuse me with lovemaking. I've got to think and I can't when you—" She broke off and looked at him with troubled eyes.

"Okay, Cassie. I think you're wrong, but I'll give you time. And we've got time—lots of it!"

The rest of the week passed swiftly. Joanna was able to put aside her reservations about the wisdom of staying on, but she couldn't quite give Travis the trust he had asked for. Barney spent a lot of time beaming from ear to ear and finding the most incredible excuses for leaving them alone at every opportunity. Joanna and Travis, amused, ignored his transparent matchmaking efforts and went on getting acquainted. They avoided the few subjects they had agreed were temporarily off-limits, but there was plenty left to talk about. She found herself falling ever more deeply in love, as Travis consciously lowered the reserve that had kept her at a distance.

Over her halfhearted objections, he gave her her first horseback riding lessons, and she found she loved it, although she paid for her pleasure with sore muscles. By Saturday she had mastered the basics, and Travis took her up on the high range for a breathtaking view of the plateau and the surrounding mountains. After their return to the ranch late in the afternoon, he offered to give her a therapeutic massage to relieve her aches and pains from the ride.

"You'll feel much better," he insisted, his mouth twisting in a wicked grin. His eyes roamed over her still-damp shoulders and the towel that was firmly tucked in over her breasts. She had just emerged from the bath and was on her way back to her room.

"I'm sure *I'd* feel better," she replied significantly, "but I don't know whether my muscles would get any benefit."

"Spoilsport. Didn't I let you fix me up with a hot pack when I was aching all over?"

"That was different." She started past him, very conscious of the inadequacies of her towel as it brushed against the top of her thighs. Not for the first time, she wished she had packed a robe in her suitcase. "You're just after revenge because you got the towel in your face, that's all."

He stopped her by planting his hand on the wall just in front of her. His face was very close as he bent over her. "No, my blue-eyed lady. That's not what I'm after," he said, his voice rumbling huskily in her ear. His breath was warm on her skin, and his tongue tantalized her as it probed the outer curve of her ear, then followed a spiraling trail into the sensitive center.

Intense pleasure radiated through her and she felt as though she were breaking a force field when she shook her head and stepped back. "You make your point very clearly," she said as lightly as she could. "But I'll never get ready for this party if you don't let me alone, Travis. Then you'll have to explain to Maggie."

"I'll explain." He bent his arm and came even closer.

"You'd better use the time for your own bath." Her nose

wrinkled as she evaded the purposeful movement of his head. "You smell like a horse!" Risking her grip on the towel, she ducked under his arm and scurried barefoot down the hall.

"Spoilsport!" he laughed again as she closed the bedroom door.

The party was in full swing when they reached the Puldowskis' two-story farmhouse. Maggie greeted Joanna with a big hug and pulled Travis down so she could reach him with a smacking kiss on the cheek.

"I'm glad you two came tonight. Where's Barney, Trav?"

"One of the horses is having a little trouble, and Barney insisted on being the one to stay behind. He'll call if Belle gets worse, so I don't know how long we can stay."

"That's too bad. You'd better start circulating, then, while you have the chance. Try some of the fancy food my daughters and I fixed up, over there on the buffet. And if you feel like dancing, the kids have got the stereo going in the playroom. Cassie, you look beautiful tonight."

Maggie's admiration was sincere, and Joanna knew she looked her best. The coral dress fit her slender body to perfection, and she had made up her eyes and face for the first time since she left the city. She had used a subtle eye shadow and silvery highlights below her brow to bring out the blue glitter of her eyes. They looked impossibly large, fringed by thick sweeping lashes. Her mouth was dewy and ripe with coral lipstick in the same shade as her dress.

Apparently Maggie had put in a good word for her among the neighbors, because most of the people who came over to greet Travis greeted her as well. Travis' obvious acceptance of her had a lot to do with the changed attitudes, she thought, though she heard one or two obliquely disapproving remarks about her staying alone in a bachelor's household.

Joanna wasn't bothered by the disapproval. She was still

glowing with the knowledge that Travis had hardly taken his eyes off her since she had walked into the living room that evening dressed for the party.

A woman in her mid-twenties with rather lank blond hair came up to them with an appealing smile for Travis and a cool one for Joanna.

"Cassie, this is Sue Ann Jackson," Travis said, smiling down at the petite woman.

"Hello. I've heard about you," Sue Ann said briefly. For a moment she looked grim as she took in the merits of the coral dress and what it was covering. By the time her eyes returned to Joanna's face framed by its cloud of gypsy curls, she looked resigned.

Joanna tried not to smile as Sue Ann made an effort to attract and hold Travis' attention. In the end, the blonde lost out to one of Maggie's granddaughters, who tugged at Travis' sleeve imploringly.

"What is it, Charlene?" he asked, bending down to pick the little girl up in his arms.

"Did your mare get her pony yet, Trav?" Charlene asked shyly in a high piping voice, twisting her finger under the tie he was wearing with a shirt and V-necked sweater.

"Sure did, honey. Only it's not a pony, it's a little filly, like you. Have your Mom bring you over soon, and you can say hello to her. Her name's Candy." Travis grinned at Joanna, and she wrinkled her nose at him.

Maggie was a good hostess, and a wily diplomat. Before the next hour had passed, many of those present who had been standoffish toward "Cassie" were quite happily telling her about community affairs and encouraging her to "stop in and see us when you're out our way."

"We meet once or twice a month," one thawed matron said, when the conversation shifted around to the activities of the local quilting society.

"If you come, I wish you'd bring Sarah's wedding ring quilt," another chimed in. "Several of our group have never seen it, and it's a remarkably fine piece of work. Do you quilt, Cassie?"

"No," Joanna responded. "But the quilts at Travis' house have given me some ideas about trying. I think it's a wonderful craft."

The first matron looked gratified. "Many people agree with you. A well-done quilt in one of the traditional patterns is worth a great deal of money these days, and there's a good market for original designs, too."

The second woman nodded in agreement. "If you're interested in joining in, just let us know. It wouldn't take long to learn, if you've got the knack and a good eye for color."

Joanna thanked the ladies for the invitation and the conversation again became general. A pang of regret passed through her at the realization that she wouldn't be here to join in, so it didn't matter how much the idea appealed to her.

A stir at the door announced a late arrival, and Joanna turned with the others to see who it was. A man of medium height, his wavy blond hair casually but expensively styled, was shaking hands with George Puldowski.

Joanna's curiosity turned to shock as the blond head turned in her direction. Metal-rimmed glasses failed to obscure the cold, hard eyes that bored into hers. She braced herself as he moved toward her through the crowd.

"Hello . . . *Cassie*," Gerald Lasker said, his smile showing even white teeth and no warmth at all. "How nice to see you again."

Her whirling wits registered the fact that he had called her Cassie. Looking down, she saw he was holding out his hand in greeting, and automatically she lifted her own hand. Instantly she regretted it. His hand tightened on hers in a crushing grip. Blood drained from her face as she stifled a cry. His eyes flared with satisfaction before he dropped her numbed fingers.

"I stopped at the ranch where you've been staying, *Cassie,* and an old geezer directed me here. I hate to be a gate-crasher, but I didn't want to miss the chance of seeing you, since I'm just passing through."

Maggie bustled over and after a doubtful look at Joanna's taut expression, spoke courteously to her uninvited guest. "Of course you're welcome, Mr. . . . Sorry, I didn't hear your name?"

"Lasker. Gerald Lasker. From Denver."

"Well, Mr. Lasker, we're pleased to have a friend of Cassie's drop in." She glanced questioningly at Travis, who had come up and was regarding the newcomer with narrow-eyed antipathy. "Why don't you find a corner somewhere and visit? I'll get one of the kids to bring you a plate of food from the buffet, and maybe a cup of coffee or a drink?"

"Thank you, Mrs. Puldowski. I'm not hungry, but a cup of coffee would be welcome." Gerald looked at Joanna as he spoke, and she knew he lied. He was hungry, but not for food.

Feeling as though she were suspended over an icy crevasse where a false move would be disastrous, Joanna was not comforted by Travis' arm encircling her waist possessively.

"Let's move over here, honey," he said. "Tommy, can we trouble you for that chair if you're not using it?"

The skinny teenager who had been hanging over a chair gawking at the stranger's elegant clothing moved away with alacrity. "Sure, Trav." He left with some other young people for the back of the house. The amplified sound of rock music reached them as a door opened and closed.

Joanna was glad to sit down; she wasn't sure how much longer her legs would have supported her. Travis and Gerald stood nearby, eyeing each other. Travis was not the least bit affected by the other man's haughtily raised eyebrow and dismissing stare.

A bubble of near-hysterical laughter threatened to erupt

from Joanna's throat; all her agonizing about confessing her identity to Travis didn't mean much now. Gerald would be only too glad to blow the whistle.

"I suppose you're the rancher *Cassie* has been living with," Gerald said nastily. "Carlyle, isn't it?"

"Cassie has been *staying* at my home. Any objections?"

"None at all. It's been some time since she and I were . . . together."

Joanna burned with resentment. Damn him! He had summed up the situation with his usual astuteness and had decided to play a little before exposing her. Or was he just trying to put her off balance so he could gain leverage for getting the lease options back? She looked up as someone came over with a tray bearing coffee cups, and groaned inwardly. It was Sally.

"Thanks, Sally," Travis said, as they each took one. No one took cream or sugar, so Sally moved away, but Joanna noted she remained well within earshot.

"Well, Cassie," Gerald began again, after another cold glance at Travis failed to make him go away, "Your friends in Denver send you their regards. Ellie was kind enough to give me your address, otherwise I probably wouldn't have been able to contact you."

"Oh?" Joanna responded blankly before she realized he must mean Kate Wilding's niece. But surely she had only mentioned a telephone number to Kate? She studied Gerald's cynical eyes, gleaming from behind his glasses. Of course. He had extracted the number from the suspicious Ellie and then traced the address; and now he was telling her so she would be intimidated by his cleverness.

"I haven't seen Donovan lately, though. He seems to have dropped out of sight. Maybe you can help me get in touch with him? Also you might be able to help me locate one or two items that have been missing since you left. They haven't turned up anywhere." His eyes were stabbing her now, and she could see his barely suppressed rage. "I hate to cause you any trouble, but I need those . . . items."

Joanna rose and placed her cup on the tray the fascinated Sally still held clasped in her arms. "I'd like to help you, Gerald, but if the items are the ones I'm thinking of, Donovan has them, and you'll have to take it up with him."

"You're certain of that?"

"Quite certain." Joanna's voice was steady and carried conviction, but Gerald regarded her with a darkening scowl.

"Well, Lasker, now that you've had your chat and your coffee, you're no doubt ready to be on your way," Travis interposed briskly. He took the cup from Gerald's hand and put it with his own on Sally's tray. "There isn't much in a community like ours to entertain men like you." The innocuous words took on insulting overtones as Travis looked Gerald up and down with glittering eyes.

Something leapt in Gerald's eyes in return. A burst of music came from the back of the house, and his thin smile appeared briefly and malevolently.

"I don't agree at all, Carlyle. I find your country gathering quite entertaining. Cassie knows I'm willing to mix with all sorts of people—don't you, my dear? I do have to be on my way, but first—how about a dance for old times' sake, Cassie? If that's dance music I hear coming from back there. Or would you rather finish our conversation here?"

Torn between a powerful impulse to tell her ex-boss to drop dead, and a dread of what his "conversation" would result in, Joanna nodded unwillingly and went along. Her feeling of impending disaster was growing stronger.

Tommy and his friends were drinking Cokes and joking together at a pool table at one end of the large room. Others were gathered around a video game in the corner. Only one couple was dancing to the beat of a slow rock ballad. Gerald pulled Joanna roughly into his arms and moved out onto the floor. Looking over his shoulder, she caught a glimpse of Travis' face as he lounged unsmiling in the doorway. The lines in his cheeks were deeply etched and his eyes were so narrowed she could hardly see the glitter anymore.

The record changed to a heavy rock beat, but the teenagers seemed to prefer the games at the other end. Gerald gripped her tighter. "This is cozy," he said, giving her another mirthless smile and ignoring her efforts to break free and dance separately. He went into a tight turn, thrusting his leg intimately between hers, and she flushed angrily.

"Stop that, Gerald," she hissed at him. "I haven't got what you want anymore, so why don't you just go?"

"But I haven't got what I want, Joanna, darling. I wanted you, remember? And you walked out on me. I didn't like that."

"You've never lacked for women, as I remember," she retorted, shoving against his chest with her elbow in an effort to put some space between them. "What's one more to you?"

"One always wants the one that got away. Especially when she's as beautiful as you. We could have done very well together, you and I, if you weren't so damned prudish."

"Particular, you mean," she snapped.

His expression turned ugly, and he danced her into a far corner. With his body shielding what he was doing, he swiftly changed his grasp to her wrist and twisted her arm around behind her back. His other hand came up to hold her head still. "You owe me, Joanna Randall," he gritted, "so start paying."

Arched against him, her arm feeling as though it were being twisted out of its socket, Joanna was helpless as he lowered his head to grind her protest into silence with his mouth. The pounding beat of the music blended with the violence of his travesty of a kiss, and tears of anger sprang into her eyes. She was about to plant the heel of her shoe in his leg when Travis' hand clamped paralyzingly on Gerald's shoulder.

"Ugh . . ." Gerald's grunt of pain was lost in the music. He released his hold on Joanna's arm, and she broke away from him. Travis squeezed a little harder and Gerald's face blanched.

"I think the lady's had enough of your kind of dancing, Lasker," Travis said through his teeth. "You don't dance any better than you shake hands. Maybe you'd better go learn some manners." With a final squeeze, he released his victim, who was no longer quite so dapper.

Shaking with rage, Gerald cradled his disabled arm. He leaned forward and said in a hate-filled voice barely covered by the music, "You've got a few things to learn yourself, Carlyle. Such as the fact that this little bitch has got you all fooled. She's not—"

"That's enough, Lasker." The menace in Travis' voice was enough to cut Gerald's words short. "One more word out of you and I'll take you outside and complete your education."

"Okay, cowboy. Have it your way. But I promise you'll regret it!" With a last virulent glance at Joanna, Gerald shoved his way out the door, almost knocking down the goggling Sally.

"Travis . . ." Joanna turned to him with relief.

"Save it, Cassie. Let's get out of here." His hand at her waist propelled her out of the playroom and into the living room.

Maggie followed them into the front hall. "Is there anything wrong, Cassie? That friend of yours took off in a hurry."

"He's not a friend, Maggie. I used to work for him." Joanna still couldn't believe it—Gerald had left without exposing her masquerade! It wasn't like him to give up so easily.

Travis retrieved their coats from the coatrack and apologized to Maggie for leaving the party early. "I'd rather not leave Barney on his own," he offered in excuse. "Belle could take a turn for the worse, and I'd rather be there just in case."

Joanna swiftly bent and kissed the older woman on the

cheek. "Thanks, Maggie, for inviting me and for seeing that I met with so much kindness. I won't forget it."

Travis whisked Joanna outside and into the truck. In a few moments, they were on the road home. The moon was obscured, and only the white swath of the headlights penetrated the darkness ahead. They traveled some miles before Travis' hands on the steering wheel relaxed their tight-knuckled grip.

"Do you want to tell me the reason for what happened back there? Or do you still not trust me?" His voice carried a strong tinge of bitterness.

"Thank you for stepping in when you did, Travis. I didn't think Gerald would try anything violent—at least not in public like that."

Travis snorted. "You told Maggie you worked for him. Who is he, and why was he manhandling you?"

"I worked for Gerald Lasker in Denver as his secretary. Those 'items' he was talking about were legal documents that belonged to someone else—not him. I took them and sent them back to the rightful owner. Gerald came after me because he thought I still had them. They're worth a lot of money."

They reached the driveway to the homestead, and Travis turned in. In a moment, they were parked at the side of the house; the motor died and he switched the lights off.

"It wasn't just documents he was after, Cassie. The bastard wanted you; I could see it. He was more to you than just your boss, wasn't he?"

"No!"

"You don't have to lie to me."

"You surely don't think I'd have anything to do with that gorilla by *choice*, do you?"

"How do I know? Women do some crazy things. I figured you had a past. Lovers, another husband before Arne, maybe, why not?" His voice sounded strained. "No man could look at you and not want you, Cassie—don't you know that?"

"Travis . . ."

"You're saucy and smart, and when you get mad your eyes shoot sparks, did you know that? When you work around the place wearing those tight jeans and thin little shirts, it's all I can do not to grab you every time I see you. Then, tonight, you come out wearing that fancy dress, looking cool and sophisticated and more beautiful than . . . I can hardly believe you're the same woman who's been cooking our meals and playing with Candy like a little kid."

With urgent hands, he slid her coat from her arms, then pulled her close; the sides of his jacket enfolded her so that she was cocooned against him and sheltered by his warmth.

"Arne, Lasker—whoever you've known, been with, wanted—whatever it is you're mixed up in, it doesn't seem to matter. I can't let you go, now. I want to make you forget there was ever anyone else . . ."

His lips moved urgently over her face, mapping her brows, her eyes, her nose, and cheeks. Joanna brought her hands up under his sweater to hold on to him. He was warm to her touch, and blindly she turned up her face, wanting him to feed the aching hunger within her.

"Come up to the house," he whispered, his lips a breath away from hers, his hands seeking her breasts, then finding them, soft and responsive to his touch. "Come with me now, Cassie, let me warm you in my bed. Warm you so that you'll forget there was ever anyone but me!"

"Oh, Travis . . ." she breathed. "I can't think . . ."

"Don't think," he lifted his head long enough to murmur raggedly. "When I hold you like this and you melt against me, I'm sure of you. It's only when you're not in my arms that I'm afraid you're not real—afraid I'll lose you. Prove to me I'm wrong! Give yourself to me, darling. I need you so."

A nameless fear curled inside her, but her heart was thundering in response to his impassioned plea. She clung to him as he helped her out of the high cab. The cold night air rushed in on them, but he kept her wrapped within his jacket and practically carried her up the veranda steps.

The grating sound of the barn door being slid back halted them at the top. Travis turned, Joanna with him, to see Barney silhouetted in a square of light.

"Travis? You'd better come quick. We've got trouble."

Chapter Eight

With a groan, Travis released her and went directly to the barn. Joanna hurried, shivering, into the house. For a moment she stood, disoriented, wanting to swear, cry out—something! She went to her room and took off her dress. It was impossible to think about quietly going to bed. The barn—she'd go see what was happening. She found her jeans and pulled them on, her wildly fluctuating emotions gradually resolving into a peculiar light-headed feeling. Relief—that's what it was, as though she'd just had a narrow escape from a trap that threatened her . . .

Travis' arms, a trap? Oh, dear heaven, I love him, don't I? Then why . . .? Her legs gave way and she slumped on the side of the bed. Oh, God, I do know why. I'll love him, give myself to him, and then he'll leave me. Reject me, just like . . .

She buried her face in her hands. That's what men did. They loved you and then they rejected you—even her own father hadn't wanted her. Why should she think Travis' claim that he cared for her meant anything different? The thought of committing herself to him was terrifying—and yet she was tempted. How she was tempted! She shuddered.

What choice do I really have? she thought bitterly. She was already trapped by loving him, knowing it would only mean an unbearable, wrenching moment of parting. It was clear now why she hadn't told him who she was long before—her identity as Cassie was the only shield she had against him. That was why she was clinging to it; she had been afraid all along—afraid to put these powerful new feelings to the test.

Her hands shaking, she rose from the bed and reached for a top. Pulling it on brought the light fabric into contact with her bare breasts, making them tingle anew, sensitized as they were from Travis' eager caresses. Her eyes closed and she remembered the touch of his hands on them. She experienced once again the delicious feelings—the promise of ecstasy . . . Stop it! she told herself, shaking her head to clear it. Don't think about what might have happened tonight!

On her way out through the kitchen, she stopped to pull on an old sweater she had seen hanging in the utility room. The sweater hung on her like a scratchy oversize sack and smelled of age, sawdust, and horses, but at least she would be warm. Her nose twitched. She doubted the remnants of her exotic perfume would overcome the sweater's earthy odor.

The barn was a darker bulk against the starlit blackness outside. A narrow crack of light showed her where the door was. She pushed it wide enough to slip inside, then closed it again to keep out the cold night air.

Travis and Barney were bent over Belle. The mare was lying on her side, her breathing labored and frightened. When Joanna approached, Travis looked up briefly, and her heart warmed at the spark of welcome she saw in his eyes before he turned his attention back to his patient.

Careful not to draw too near and get in the way, Joanna sat on a bale of straw and drew up her feet. She pulled the rough sweater down over her knees and hugged her arms around them. Watching Travis as he spoke to Belle in low comforting tones, his face intent and compassionate, she felt an uprush of emotion. She loved him so much—could she bear to give him up?

Poor Belle whinnied fearfully and Joanna's attention focused on the mare. She was ashamed that she hadn't given much thought to Belle's plight, or to little Candy, very quiet in a corner of the next stall.

"Are we going to lose her, Trav?" Barney's voice was worried.

"Not if I can help it. You should have called earlier."

"Didn't hear the truck come in. I was going up to the house to phone Maggie's when I saw you."

"It's too late to get Baxter out here. I'll have to do what I can. Cassie, you'd better go back to the house."

"I'd rather stay. Maybe there'll be something I can do to help."

He didn't argue, just got busy with some heavy tubing and an ominous array of equipment. The next couple of hours were full of activity for all of them. Before they were done, Joanna was on her knees holding Belle's head and uttering disjointed soothing words of encouragement to the mare.

Finally Travis told her and Barney there was nothing else for them to do. "The medication is taking effect now; I think she'll be all right. I'll stay a while longer just in case. There are some blankets in the tack room. It wasn't exactly what I planned on tonight, but . . ."

He looked at Joanna ruefully and she grinned back at him, suddenly conscious of their appearance. They were all filthy. She looked down; the sweater was a write-off. What a change from the way they had looked at the party!

Travis bent over her suddenly and kissed her swiftly and possessively on her weary mouth. "You darling," was all he said. But his eyes were diamond-bright.

Disoriented again, Joanna could barely stammer out a good night to Barney before making her way back to the house, stumbling twice on the way.

The following morning, tired but triumphant, the three of them celebrated Belle's recovery over a breakfast of thick slices of ham and hot pancakes with blueberry syrup. Barney's face wore a perpetual sly grin as he heartily made a dent in the stack of tender cakes, and Joanna knew he was congratulating himself on the success of his matchmaking. What else could he think, after that kiss?

Before she sat down at the table, she had been conscious of Travis studying her closely. The short-sleeved top she was wearing was blue, the same shade as her eyes, and when he frowned, she wondered why. True, the top was a bit tight, but . . .

"You don't have many clothes with you, do you?"

"Well, no, but—"

"I noticed you were wearing my old sweater last night." He smiled suddenly. "Definitely not your style. You're going to need something better than that for cool weather."

Joanna smiled back and reached out to replenish Barney's coffee cup. "I only brought one suitcase with me, and the rest of my things are . . . in storage."

"You could send for your things."

"I suppose I could . . ." she replied slowly, trying not to show her fear, knowing he was asking her to commit herself.

He studied her face for a moment, then nodded. "There's no rush. I'll have to stay close to Belle today, but you could come into town with me tomorrow and pick up a few things you might need to get by with. Then decide later about the rest."

"That's a great idea, Cassie," Barney chipped in. "One thing you need is a pair of boots. Tennis shoes are no good for riding. You'll want to go out again now you've got the hang of it. Travis, you ought to take her over by Jackson's Rock, where the stream is. Mighty pretty around there.''

"If the horse is willing to put up with me, I'd like another ride. But I'd rather not go too far or too fast. Okay, Travis?''

"I'll let you set the pace, Cassie, until you're more confident.'' The glint in his gray eyes acknowledged her retreat. His fleeting smile told her he didn't intend to let her retreat very far.

The following day, Monday morning, Travis drove her into town. Prospect did not exactly bustle, but it did boast a respectable Main Street. The shops and stores were more than adequate to serve the basic needs of a widespread farming and ranching community.

"It looks like the universal form of transportation around here is the pickup truck,'' she observed as they pulled up and parked in an empty space near a two-story department store. There were two or three other pickups parked along the street.

"Winters here are hard on autos. Unless a man has a large family, it's handier all around to use a truck. I could afford to run more than one vehicle, but I haven't needed to . . . until now.''

The implication of "until now" left Joanna speechless. He certainly was making clear to her the direction his thoughts were taking for the future. His eyes showed his amusement at her confusion. He picked up her hand and raised it, palm upward, and she felt the swift hard pressure of his lips. He folded her fingers carefully over his kiss and smiled at her.

"I'll leave the truck here and walk on over to the veterinarian's office in the next street. I think you should be able to find most things right here, and there's a good boot shop a couple of doors down. You can put your purchases in the storage box behind the seat if you want to explore before I get back. Are you sure you have enough money?''

"Plenty, thanks." She patted her purse, which contained the generous wages he had given to her before they left the ranch. She was still rather shaken by his confident assumption they had a future. That reference to a large family . . .

"I'll check back in an hour or so, then maybe we can have lunch?" He came around and helped her down from the cab. "You've got your choice of tacos or Chinese or hamburgers."

"That's what I like—international cuisine!"

Joanna visited the boot shop first. The pair she settled on were a good fit, western, with slanted thick heels and a minimum of tooling on the honey-tan leather. Though the clerk tried to tell her they weren't the best thing for walking, she handed him her tennis shoes to wrap and kept the boots on. Pleased with her purchase, she tried not to admit to herself that it was a first step toward the commitment she was so afraid of. She stepped lightly as she left the shop, turned toward the department store, and collided with a man who was standing just outside.

"Oh! Pardon me," she murmured automatically, putting up her hand to catch her balance. Hard eyes glinted at her through metal-framed glasses. "Gerald!" she exclaimed.

"I've been waiting to talk to you." Her ex-boss grasped her elbow in a grip she knew he would not relinquish without a scene. "You saved me a trip back up the mountain today."

"I have nothing to say to you, Gerald," she declared hotly.

"I'd think twice about that. I just might have a talk with the local law instead; I doubt if you'd like that."

Joanna was fed up. She looked around and saw a small public square built around a civic statue half a block away. "Let's go down there." She nodded toward the square. "Maybe I do have something to say. After you've heard it, you can do what you like."

Soon they were sitting side by side on a wooden bench

next to a bed of colorful petunias. A flowering shrub partially obscured them from the main street. Joanna took a deep breath.

"Okay, Gerald," she said, starting with what would concern him most. "You want those options. I'll save you some time by saying again I don't have them." She raised her hand to halt his explosive objection. "I mailed them to Donovan several days ago. He's bound to have them by now, so it's no use you hanging around menacing me. I doubt you'd like to explain in detail just how you came to get those leases in the first place. Don't you think it's time to cut your losses?"

Something violent flickered in the pale eyes behind the glasses, then Gerald laughed. "You're not afraid of me, are you, Joanna? You know, I really am sorry we didn't get together. We would have made a helluva team."

"You would have hated it. I can be a real nag when I don't like something. And with you, I didn't find a whole lot to like," she told him candidly.

He leaned back and crossed his legs, neatly adjusting the crease in his slacks. His shoes gleamed with reflected sunlight. The light wasn't kind to his face—she couldn't help comparing his unhealthy color with Travis' tanned good looks. The hand that rested on Gerald's knee was soft and thick; her own taste ran to lean, strong hands with tapered, callused fingers.

"It wasn't your liking I was after." His eyes hardened. "But let's get back to business. I stand to lose a lot of money if I don't get those options back by next Monday. You know where Donovan is. Tell him I'm willing to make a deal with him. Persuade the old crock to come out in the open, and I'll let you off the hook."

Joanna was already shaking her head. "No dice. I sent those papers to a post office box. Your men followed Donovan to a lawyer's office, remember? You can try contacting him through the lawyer—if you still want to."

"You're lying," Gerald accused, uncrossing his legs and

leaning forward, his hands clenched on his knees, now uncaring of the creases. "You know where Donovan is, and if you don't do what I want, I'll make sure you regret it. You've got something going with the cowboy, haven't you? I could tell him quite a story about how Joanna Randall left Lasker Development under a cloud. Better yet, I could tell him about the mink coat and the apartment I paid for."

"I never took so much as a paper clip from you—and if you invent some silly story about a love nest . . ."

"Ah, but Travis won't think it's silly. Lovers are notoriously jealous. I doubt he's any different."

Was Gerald right? It would be difficult enough to explain the truth about herself to Travis; if he heard Gerald's distorted story—well, who knew? She hid her apprehension.

"I don't think you can count on that," she bluffed. "Travis might surprise you. He doesn't like bullies, as you learned the other night. And he has a strong protective instinct where I'm concerned. I wouldn't tangle with him, if I were you." She stood up and looked down at Gerald scornfully. "In any case, you can't intimidate me."

Her adversary stood as well, his expression ugly. Aware that he was on the verge of violence, Joanna got ready to run. Then a wave of relief overtook her. Over Gerald's shoulder she saw Travis striding toward them. Her widening eyes must have given Gerald warning, for he turned sharply. His head snapped up when he saw Travis. Hastily he stepped backward, his foot coming down hard on Joanna's instep.

"Owww!" she cried, tears springing to her eyes at the sudden sharp pain. Travis leapt forward. Joanna hopped about in anguish, reaching for her injured foot with one hand. Unused to the western boots, she lost her balance and fell backward just as Travis reached them.

"Cassie!" he exclaimed as she cried out again. "Darling, are you hurt?"

Since she had landed on her fanny, it was mostly her

pride that was damaged. But then she saw a long scratch right across the smooth expensive leather of her new boots. ''Oh, damn!'' she wailed. ''Gerald, you beast!''

Misunderstanding her cry of dismay, Travis drew his long arm back and his hand formed into a lethal fist. Gerald paled and scrambled hastily backward. Jerking his head to one side at the last second, he managed to evade the punch.

''Dammit, Carlyle, I didn't do anything to her!'' he yelled, almost tripping over Joanna.

''Look out,'' Joanna cried, twisting to avoid getting stepped on again. Over her head she saw Travis' second roundhouse swing miss the blond head by a slender margin. The metal glasses went askew. Gerald put his fists up defensively, but looked wildly about for an avenue of escape. Unable to get to her feet with the men scrambling around her, Joanna saw the funny side of the fight that wasn't quite happening. Her gurgle of laughter turned into a sharp cry as Gerald tripped over her and his shoe connected painfully with her ribs.

''Ouch! Gerald!''

''Watch out, Cassie!'' Travis exclaimed as he redoubled his efforts to nail the slippery Gerald, trying to edge him away from her. ''Stand still, dammit! What kind of man are you? Do you only fight with women?''

Gerald apparently decided desperate situations required desperate solutions. He vaulted over the bench, landed in a rolling fall in the bed of petunias, scrambled to his feet, and bolted. The last Joanna saw of him was the back of his custom-made suit, now liberally and colorfully streaked with dirt and mashed petunias.

The petunias were the last straw. Holding her sides, she gasped as Travis dropped to his knees beside her. His arms surrounded her; his voice was sharp with anxiety.

''Sweetheart, what is it? Where do you hurt?''

''In my . . . in my rib cage. Oh, Travis, if I laugh any more I think I'll die. . . .'' She put her arms around him and felt the pounding of his heart as he anxiously passed his hands over her. Then her laughter ended, and she was clinging to him and feeling another emotion entirely.

She buried her face in the juncture of his throat and shoulder, breathing in an acrid, musky scent. Hazily she knew it was the smell of the adrenaline-charged force of his anxiety for her and of his anger against the man he thought was harming her. She pressed her lips to his moist skin with fervent passion. A wave of love for him swept through her, and she tightened her arms around his body with all her strength.

When he felt the force of her embrace, his hands stilled. He looked into the yearning face she raised to him. Their lips met in a clumsy, urgent kiss. His arms locked about her, straining her willing body to his. She felt his heartbeat as if it were her own and gave herself over to his kiss.

Finally their embrace loosened and gentled. They stared at each other, and awareness dawned on them both: they were in a public park, putting on an exhibition that could get them arrested. Joanna began to smile, and then to laugh softly.

"So help me, Cassie," Travis' mouth twisted crookedly, as he released her. "Are you laughing again?" He got to his feet and helped her to stand. They looked around sheepishly. At least no crowd had gathered, Joanna thought thankfully, though she did hear sounds of people talking not far away.

"Thank God it's not Saturday," Travis said. "Let's get out of here." He put his arm around her waist and started to lead her from the square.

"Where are we going?" she asked, picking up the package containing her tennis shoes. Surely he was going to ask for some explanation of what she had been doing with Gerald, or—or something! "Don't you want to talk about this?"

"I think we'd better not push our luck. It'll hold until we

get back to the ranch. There I can guarantee privacy, and believe me, privacy is necessary for what I have in mind.''

"Travis . . .'' she said doubtfully.

"Please, Cassie,'' he said. "We'll talk about it, I promise you.''

They stopped at the truck just as a car pulled alongside. John Temple's face appeared next to his daughter's on the passenger side as he leaned over to speak to Travis through the open window.

"Trav, I'm glad I caught you. Sally said she saw you in town. Abbott's here, and he's agreed to meet with us tonight. If we want to have a say in that new water-rights legislation, we'd better see to it he understands our side of it. I've called the others, and they'll be at my place this afternoon. Can you come over now? We can hash over the arguments and be ready for Abbott tonight. What do you say?''

"Are you sure you need me, John? If the rest of you—''

"You know how hard he is to convince, Trav. He listened to you last time. We need you to persuade him we ranchers on the slope have got as much to complain about as they have in the flatlands. We've got to stick together on this. We need that legislation.''

"Okay, John.'' Gray eyes flickered to Joanna in silent apology. "Who else is coming?''

The rancher plunged into a recitation of names of the other men he had contacted. Joanna turned her attention to Sally, sitting silently in her dad's car. Her eyes were red-rimmed, her mouth pursed tightly as though she were struggling to keep from crying.

Joanna had an uncomfortable flash of intuition. Sally had told her father she'd seen Travis. Sally could have seen Travis on the path with her—seen their embrace. Poor Sally. She was getting initiated into adulthood the hard way.

"Okay, John.'' Travis concluded the discussion with his

neighbor. "I'll drive Cassie home now and come over to your place right away."

When the Temples had gone, Travis turned to Joanna, his mouth twisting regretfully. "There goes our day, I'm afraid. You didn't get much shopping done, honey. Do you mind making it another time?"

"Of course not. Let's get on back to the ranch. These boots cost me enough for one trip, anyway." She lifted a foot for him to admire. "Neat, aren't they?"

"Beautiful," he replied, smiling into her eyes. He opened the door and helped her into the truck. After taking his own seat and starting the motor, he said offhandedly, "There's something for you behind the seat."

With a questioning look, she turned and drew out a bulky package. Careful not to get in the way of the steering wheel as they drove through town, she unwrapped the package and discovered a butter-soft sheepskin jacket inside.

"Travis!"

His eyes reflected satisfaction as he glanced at the soft fur she was holding to her cheek. "Winter's coming on," he said, "and I'll be wearing my old sweater when I'm stacking wood, so you'll need this."

His look was enough to warm her, she thought. There was no doubt he believed she would be here when winter came.

"Travis . . ." She was about to protest further, but he interrupted: "Consider it a bonus, if you like, for all the hard work you've put in; or as an apology for the way I treated you when you first came. I had hoped we'd be able to talk this afternoon at lunch, but now it looks like I'll be tied up all day. I can't let the others down, sweetheart."

"I understand. Don't worry about it. I had a fun morning, anyway."

They both laughed and he patted her knee. They turned onto the canyon road and began their upward climb. Joanna stroked the soft creamy sheepskin, touched by his gesture as well as his apology. Would he regret the apology when he heard what she had to say a little later? She couldn't hide behind her shield any longer. If only she could believe in the picture of herself still here when the snows came, wearing his gift . . .

"Cassie . . ." he began after a period of thoughtful silence on both their parts. "You know I want to make love to you."

Her heart leapt in response. "Yes, Travis, I know it."

"If you're afraid that's all it is . . ."

"No. No, I'm not afraid of that." She was not entirely sure it was the truth, but she said it anyway.

"I've been as patient as I could. It's been hard because I feel so sure you want it, too, whether you admit it or not. What are you afraid of? Was it something that happened between you and Arne? Or something that happened with this guy Gerald Lasker?"

"There was nothing between Gerald and me, Travis. Not like he made it sound."

Travis glanced at her, frowning, before looking back at the road. "That Lasker is bad news. He ran today, but he could be dangerous on his own ground. If he's got you mixed up in something crooked . . ."

"No, nothing like that. He's everything you said, but he has no real hold over me."

"You're an independent kind of woman, aren't you? You hate to admit you've gotten in over your head. I figure you were in some kind of trouble when you married Arne, but he died and you were on your own again. You let him help you; won't you let me do as much? Can't you give up some of that independence and let me in on what's troubling you?"

Joanna hugged the jacket to her body in spite of the warmth of the midday heat, cherishing the comfort of his gift. The warm, protective tones of his voice reached a hurting, empty place inside her. It had been so long since she'd believed there could ever be anything like that kind of caring—she'd lost it all so early in her life. She'd learned to live without it. Did she dare reach out for it now? Risk suffering the pain of loss again?

"Darling?" he prompted gently.

"What if you don't like what you hear, Travis?" she asked him. She looked up with a painful twist to her mouth; he glanced down again and their eyes met.

His hands shifted on the wheel. "If I've come to terms with the fact that you were Arne's wife, I guess I can come to terms with anything. I care about you and I think you care about me, too. But I need to hear it from you, Cassie."

She started to blurt out the bottom line—that she was not Cassie—then closed her mouth again. There wasn't enough time; she'd botch it, and it was crucial that he understand clearly how it had all come about. She chose her next words carefully, knowing she was at last making her commitment to him.

"Travis, I do care. I care a great deal." She placed her hand on his knee, and his hand dropped to cover it and squeeze hard before returning to the steering wheel. "There are a number of things I want to tell you, and I agree that we need time and privacy to discuss them." She hesitated for a moment, debating. Perhaps she could pave the way for what would come later.

"There is one thing I want you to know now. About Arne. You say it bothers you, thinking about me being with him. Well, I was never his wife; I never slept with him."

The truck screeched to a halt. Travis turned toward her, his eyes blazing. "Is that the truth?" he asked, searching her face.

"Yes."

His taut frame sank back against the seat. "Thank God! Cassie, you don't know . . ." He reached out, clasped her head between his hands, and drew her toward him for a long hard kiss. Releasing her, he smiled warmly, dissolving her last doubts. "None of the rest makes any difference now. We can handle it, you and I together." He restarted the motor and with a look invited her to move closer to him.

Joanna put the jacket away carefully and changed her position. She tucked her legs under her and curved an arm around him so that she was as close as she could get without interfering with his driving. She felt as though she had just fallen from a great height and had landed on her feet, as if . . . No, there weren't words to express what she was feeling, she decided happily. She was actually looking forward to the conversation ahead. It was going to work out all right!

Travis turned his head and gave her a quick kiss. By this time they had left the winding portion of the road behind. Joanna risked a nibbling kiss on the vulnerable spot just behind his earlobe. His hand dropped to her thigh, and she stopped nibbling, afraid she had distracted him from his driving.

He growled huskily, "Don't stop, honey. Have you any idea how good that feels?"

"Mmm-hmm," she murmured, returning her attention to the sensitive spot she had located. With the tip of her tongue, she explored the spot further. She slid one hand between the buttons of his shirt. His hand tightened convulsively on her thigh.

His voice sounded a bit strangled when he said, "John had better appreciate the sacrifice I'm making by coming to talk to that damned politician. If it weren't for . . . Mmm—honey, I guess you'll have to stop that."

Reluctantly she drew away from him and prudently resumed her former place on the passenger side, rubbing her thigh. "Maybe you're right. I can't afford any more bruises. First the horseback riding, then falling on my backside, and now you and your roaming hands."

His eyes blazed like gray diamonds. "Honey, what I'd like to do with my hands doesn't bear talking about right now. But later . . ."

The promise in his voice thrilled her. She smiled at him, a little nervous—impatient for the explanations to be done with and longing for the night to come.

Chapter Nine

Joanna turned dejectedly away from the telephone. It was just too much! She'd spent the afternoon in a state of nervous anticipation, and now Travis wasn't going to be home until much later—possibly not until morning.

"Blast!" she muttered out loud, looking with disgust at the beautifully set table. The best linens, the china and silver—she'd wanted everything to be perfect. Reluctantly she removed one setting. Well, she told herself, at least Barney would enjoy the roast beef and Yorkshire pudding she had prepared. She tried to put on a happy face when he came in a few minutes later, but he wasn't fooled.

"What's wrong, Cassie? You look lower than a hound-dog with a sore nose. Didn't you have a good time in town today? Where's Trav?"

"He just called a few minutes ago. He had to go to the Temple ranch to meet with the other ranchers. Some politician named Abbott was supposed to be there, but he's been delayed."

Barney nodded. "That'd be Henry Abbott. The ranchers

around here have been anxious to get in touch with him about water rights. That's one of the troubles in this state. Some have the water, but most don't. Pretty hard to figure how to share it around fairly. Guess they'll be talking late into the night over there.''

"Travis said he'd probably stay over, and for us not to wait up for him." Though he hadn't been able to say much over the phone, his voice had told her he was as disappointed as she was.

"Well, Cassie, I guess we can find something to pass the time, can't we?" Barney spoke heartily, his eyes sympathetic. Throughout the meal, he exerted himself to bolster her spirits. He complimented her on her cooking, her new boots, persuaded her to try on the sheepskin jacket so he could see how she looked in it, and generally built her up until she called a halt, laughing.

"Okay, Barney," she said, "why don't we relax for an hour or so in the living room. I'd like to read some more in Sarah Carlyle's book, and I'll bet you haven't finished those magazines that came in the mail last week. What do you say?"

"Sounds good to me."

They settled down to read for the rest of the evening. After a while, Joanna let the chintz-covered book fall into her lap. The women who had compiled these recipes were strong women, she decided. How often their strength had been tested. Skimpy notes here and there gave clues that revealed how the everyday things that built up a life were interwoven with the sadness and tragedies that came to tear it down. She read again a note in the margin of a recipe for a kind of old-fashioned brownie cookie: "Dear Charlie's favorite cookie. How can I ever bake them again, knowing he's gone? This terrible, terrible war." A date followed: May 27, 1918, and the initials 'M.C.' Travis' great-grandmother, Joanna guessed.

There was another carefully preserved entry: a handwritten invitation to a wedding. Folded inside was a sketch of the decorations for a wedding cake. On the back of the sketch was noted: "The cake turned out well. Everyone pleased. The new addition to the house finished in time for the wedding. Sarah will be a good daughter-in-law, I think. I pray they will have fine children, and be happy." Another hand had added, "Prayer answered! S.C."

Tears misted Joanna's eyes. To be a part of this family would be a fine thing, she thought. How wonderful to have children here in the mountains where they could explore and climb and run free. With a father like Travis, a tall man with a narrow face that could light up with love and win your heart with a look. Who would ride with, and teach, and protect his own at whatever cost to himself. Little Charlene, Maggie's granddaughter, had recognized the tender, caring man behind the reserve that could keep adults at a distance. What would he be like with a daughter of his own? Never, never would he leave a child of his to grow up as best she could in an impersonal, often cruel environment.

"Travis," she whispered, longing for him to be there with every fiber of her being. She felt intensely vulnerable now that she had committed herself to him. How often, in the past, she had moved on before she could become too attached to anyone or anyplace. Friends, yes, she had had those. But no one she had minded saying good-bye to—with fondness, sometimes a little regret—but good-bye nevertheless. Now her heart had caught her off guard and had begun to put down tiny roots. She supposed the restlessness that had kept her moving had really been a kind of search; she just hadn't realized it.

She curled deeper into the soft cushions of the couch, and a piece of notepaper fell out of the book. It was a record of a meeting of the local quilting society; it mentioned Sarah Carlyle as being appointed to deal with correspondence from a museum about acquiring some examples of local quilting.

Joanna's mouth indented at the corners. If she were to

make up a quilt to represent her generation, would it include pieces bearing a happy sun face and a rainbow leading to a pot of gold? The quilts in the chest and on the beds were representative of the worn-out clothing of other generations, so why not the T-shirts of today in the quilts of tomorrow? The problem would be the fabric. It was too light. What she'd have to do was . . .

With an idea for a modern quilt design germinating in her mind, she put the diary-cookbook away and went to bed, dreamily saying good night to Barney on the way.

When she woke the next morning, with that pleasant feeling of something wonderful about to happen, she stretched her arms wide welcoming the sun streaming into the room. Absently she mused that she would have to see about getting some curtains soon. She jumped out of bed and hurried to dress. Perhaps Travis had come home last night after all.

His bed hadn't been slept in. Disappointed, she curbed her impatience. Maybe he'd be here in time for breakfast. No, Maureen and Sally wouldn't let him go without eating at their place. Drat.

Barney's breakfast that morning was not up to her usual standards, but he didn't complain when she handed him a plate of bacon that was partly burnt, and eggs that were firm and brown around the edges instead of sunny-side up. There was an understanding twinkle in his eye. Before he left, he said: "I'll be around for lunch, Cassie. I've got to fix the postholer, so mostly I'll be in the machine shop. But don't bother to cook me anything. I'll heat up some chili."

"Oh, Barney," she exclaimed in dismay. "I'm sorry about your breakfast. I'll do better at lunch."

"No," he insisted. "You and Trav need this time for yourselves. I'm not blind, you know. Why don't you fix up a picnic and ride over to Jackson's Rock when he gets back?"

"Maybe we will. I'll see what Travis says." Barney's

satisfied expression made her add, "Why do I have a feeling Jackson's Rock is the local Lovers' Lane—Mr. Matchmaker?"

Barney rubbed the back of his neck, giving her a look of assumed innocence. "It's awfully pretty up there—flowers and all," he said vaguely.

"Oh, Barney, I hope it'll work out."

"It will, honey, it will."

Then the waiting began again. After seeing to the horses, Joanna prepared a picnic lunch, glancing frequently at the clock. Surely Travis would be along soon. In the storeroom getting some apples, she smiled as she remembered the first kiss they had shared there. The sound of someone entering from the veranda brought her out of her daydream. Her heart beating faster, she hurried back to the kitchen.

The smile of greeting that lit her face quickly changed to shocked concern. Travis' face was taut and almost gray beneath his tan. His eyes were blazing. His right hand was clenched into a fist, crushing several sheets of paper and a torn envelope.

"Travis! What is it? What's the matter?" She ran to him, her hands extended.

"You lied to me." His voice was so bitterly harsh it stopped her as though she had run into a brick wall. "All this time, you've been lying to me!"

Joanna recoiled, her hands falling to her side. "Oh, no . . ." she whispered in shock.

"Right from the start I suspected something, but like a fool I let you get to me. I *wanted* not to find anything wrong with you—I let Barney talk me out of checking up on you in Denver. I just thought you were in trouble, but I never thought you'd . . . Like a blind, stupid fool, I . . ." he choked.

She stared at him in horror. It was too late. Gerald had taken his revenge after all.

"You found out?" she asked through a throat that was so

tight she could hardly get out the words. "What did he tell you?"

He ignored her questions, just looking at the papers he was crushing in his hand as though he could hardly believe they were there. "We didn't stop and pick up the mail yesterday. We were too caught up in . . ." He paused, then corrected himself: "*I* was too caught up in a state where I wasn't thinking any too clearly. But you were calculating just how thoroughly you had me wrapped around your little finger, weren't you?"

"That's not true. I'm sorry I deceived you, but—"

"Then you admit it? You planned the whole thing from the first?"

"Well, yes, but the way it happened wasn't that simple. When you came into the bus station, I . . ." Fear beat wings inside her breast. He wasn't listening; a light in the back of his eyes had gone out, as though her words had quenched his last spark of belief in her.

"Travis, darling, please listen to me. I can't explain how it happened if you look at me like that, as though you hated me. Whatever Gerald told you, can't you wait to hear my side before you judge me?"

"So he was in this, too, was he? How many others? You and Lasker, your friend Donovan. I heard you myself, on the phone, heard you say that things hadn't gone like you expected, and how you'd get the papers to him for the lawyer. And then the woman, of course—you certainly needed her for your plans. How many people do you have to share the payoff with?"

"What payoff? What are you talking about?"

Travis opened his fist and let the papers fall to the floor. He took a step toward her, his lips drawn back in a twisted grimace, and, her worst nightmare coming true before her eyes, she watched him look at her in just that way she had feared he would when he knew . . .

"Oh, God, no," she said, despairing. She retreated from

him until her back was against the counter, her head pressed against the cabinet overhead. He followed her and his hands hit the cabinets on both sides of her head, blocking her in; she could feel the heat from his body as he leaned against her. His eyes scorched her with another kind of heat.

"Your face is so fresh and open, *sweetheart*. No hard lines, no way to tell that behind the face is a scheming mind that can take a man for everything he has—and then go on to rob him after he's dead."

"I didn't—"

"Oh, yes, *darling*. You wanted to make sure there were no hitches in your scheme, no interference, didn't you? You came up here, all wide eyes and willing hands, to soften me up so I wouldn't contest the transfer. How you must have laughed when I told you there was nothing here for you. And all the time you knew about the annuity."

"Stop it!" she moaned, turning her head away. The look in his eyes as he called her sweetheart, and darling, in that terrible, sarcastic voice, was tearing her apart.

Hard fingers on her chin forced her to look back at him. "Where did you get the baby? And don't try to tell me it's really yours."

Joanna's eyes went huge. "Baby?" Had his brain snapped?

He stood away from her and scooped the crumpled papers from the floor. Contemptuously he dropped them on the counter beside her. "From the maternity hospital. The bills are all here, sent to me as executor of Arne's estate. So where is the heir I'm supposed to turn the annuity over to? Naturally as the baby's 'mother,' you'll be the guardian of the money. But if Lasker's your partner as well as your lover, I don't think fifty thousand will go very far: he looks like he's got expensive tastes. How did you set it up? Did you find some poor girl in trouble and offer to pay her medical expenses if she'd use Arne's name on the birth certificate?"

"Are you out of your mind, Travis?" Joanna exclaimed

fiercely. "I don't know anything about a baby, or hospital bills, or—"

"Give it up, will you? And don't bother flashing those blue eyes at me—it won't work anymore. You've fed me one lie after another: like the one about never sleeping with Arne! Did you have to lie about that just to set me up for a patsy?"

Corrosive like acid, the words came pouring out of him, full of anger. And under the anger—a terrible pain that matched her own. She had to stop him. He had to listen to her!

"No, Travis—I lied to you, yes, but only about—"

He cut her off. "Well, the game's over. Finished. You can go back to Lasker now, and settle whatever the quarrel was between you. If you want to fight for the money, you can talk to my lawyer." Turning on his heel, Travis walked heavily to the door.

"Where are you going?" she cried.

With his hand on the screen door, he turned his head slightly, not looking at her. "You can tell Barney that I'm going with the committee to register a formal protest about the water dispute. I'm riding over to meet John now. I don't know when I'll be back." His head turned fully toward her. Pain glazed the gray eyes, but his face was set and hard. "I want you out of my house, Cassie. Barney will drive you into town. Just . . . be gone when I get back."

"I don't understand—there's some mistake, Travis! Wait, you've got to listen!"

"Good-bye, Cassie," he said roughly. He went down the veranda steps two at a time as though pursued by devils.

Freed from the shock that held her, Joanna ran after him. "Damn you, Travis! Come back here, you blind, hardheaded . . ." Her cry ended as she choked on the words. Through her tears she saw him reach the barn and mount his horse. Stumbling down the steps, she tripped and fell on the path. Dazed, she could only think No, no, no . . .

The sound of galloping hooves told her he had left. And the pain began. Overwhelming waves of pain. It had happened after all, just as she had known it would.

"What did I do that was so terrible?" she whispered, her fingers clutching a clump of dried grass. "I didn't mean any harm."

Wiping the tears from her face, she sat up, not caring that she had grazed her arm. Then she stood up, not looking back at the house. She couldn't bear to go inside again, not with the dreams she had spun about her place there with Travis. She heard whining mechanical noises coming from the machine shop, knew Barney was there, but turned away and began to run.

Time lost its meaning, but finally her wanderings brought her to the one place that was not tied up with her memories of Travis: Barney's cabin. Tiredly she climbed the steps and sat down in one of the rustic chairs on the small front porch. She closed her eyes. When she opened them a little later, it was to see Barney looking down at her anxiously.

"Oh, Barney!" she cried brokenly. She jumped to her feet and threw her arms around him.

He held her and patted her shoulder. "There now, honey," he said gruffly, clearing his throat. "It isn't as bad as all that. Nothing that can't be fixed, I'm sure."

Drawing back, Joanna wiped the corners of her eyes with both hands and sank down in the chair. "Oh, yes, it is," she said drearily. "You don't know just how mixed-up everything is."

He sat down in the other chair beside her. "Well, I know that you aren't Cassie Carlyle."

"You do?" she stared at him, astonished. "How did you find out? I thought Travis knew, but when I tried to explain, he started accusing me of trying to claim Arne's money by using somebody's baby! Then he called me Cassie again, and stormed out. I just don't understand!"

He regarded her thoughtfully for a moment. "So that's what the boy thought, was it?" He sighed. "Well, I guess things are kind of mixed-up, at that. We'll just have to see what we can do to straighten them out.''

"Nothing can straighten this out. Travis—"

"Trav has a hasty temper, that's all. If he'd taken a little more time to think it out . . . It took me a while to figure it out, myself. Those bills on the counter—I saw the name on them, and the dates. That's when I knew you couldn't be Cassie. You aren't, are you?"

"No. I'm Joanna Randall. I . . . just let everyone think I was Cassie.''

"I think you'd better tell me how you came to do that, don't you? Are you a friend of hers?"

"No. I just happened to be in the bus station when Travis came to pick her up. He mistook me for her, and I needed a place to go. Oh, Barney, at the time I thought it was a godsend!''

As briefly as she could, jumbling up the sequence of events in her agitation, Joanna described how she came to be in the bus station that night four weeks before. Barney's face was rapt with interest as he listened.

". . . so I grabbed the papers and ran. If the man who had come to the hotel to meet Gerald hadn't seen me, they wouldn't have known who took them. I knew I didn't have much time, but I took a chance and went back to my apartment and threw some things in a suitcase. I didn't have much money—my paycheck was due the next week, and I'd loaned—well, I didn't have much money on me. Donovan wasn't at his place, and I was afraid to keep trying to reach him by phone. I thought if I could just get away somewhere, buy some time to sort things out . . .''

Barney broke in, clenching his fists on his knees, "I didn't like the looks of that fellow when he came to the ranch looking for you. He said you used to work for him. I figured it wouldn't do any harm to send him over to George and Maggie's, but I'm sorry I did, now.''

"It wouldn't have made any difference. He was hunting for me, and I knew it was only a matter of time before he found me. I tried to put him off the track. I even tried to disguise myself: I borrowed a coat and scarf from my landlady to make myself a little less conspicuous.''

''Hard to do,'' Barney smiled a little. ''You stand out in a crowd, honey, as pretty as you are.''

Joanna's smile was a bit strained. ''Anyway, it didn't make any difference in the end. He found me through the telephone number I gave Donovan.''

''Why didn't you tell us, Joanna? When you got to know us better?''

''That's a little hard to answer, Barney. I don't know if I can explain it, but at first I was just trying to keep from complicating your lives any more than I had already, and then . . . Well, then I was afraid of Travis hating me, and I just couldn't . . . Oh, Barney!'' She buried her face in her hands. ''It's no use. Travis despises me. I never should have stayed on; I knew it wouldn't work.''

''What'd you do to your arm?'' Barney reached out to take her hand and examine her injury. Dried blood and dust caked the long graze. ''Come inside, I'll fix it up for you.''

''But, Barney, you haven't explained about Arne and the money . . .'' she protested as he helped her rise from the chair.

''I will. Let's have a cup of tea. I think I understand how Travis got things mixed up.''

While Barney located a basin of water and a first-aid kit Joanna looked around the main room of his cabin. There was a comfortable-looking couch and chairs, and a small stereo system in a cabinet. Wood-carving tools and odd pieces of wood were laid out neatly on a table by a window, and, arranged in an informal gallery, framed photographs hung on the wall opposite the entrance.

''Let's have a look at that arm now.'' Carefully Barney washed away the grit and blood while Joanna tried not to wince.

She looked away and her eyes were caught by one of the photographs. It was a snapshot of a boy with a narrow face and a wide grin—Travis, of course. He was proudly standing beside a healthy-looking steer with a large ribbon attached to the harness around its neck, describing it as GRAND CHAMPION, 4-H, along with a date. The young Travis couldn't have been more than thirteen, she guessed.

There were pictures of another boy, a fresh-faced boy with sandy hair and freckles. That must be Arne, she decided, studying the youthful face with interest. There were shots of the boys together, in different stages of growth, one of Barney and a tall man who looked vaguely like Travis, and several of a woman who could only be Travis' mother, Sarah. In one of the pictures, she was laughing, her narrow face alight with the same unforgettable look Joanna had seen in Travis' face when he had smiled at her.

Barney stood up and gathered the things he had brought in. "There, now, that's fixed your arm. Let's have that cup of tea and see what we can do about straightening things out between you and Travis."

"Are you sure you should, Barney? After all, I lied to you both; at least, I didn't object when everyone took it for granted I was Cassie. And, even if those lease options did belong to Donovan, I stole them from Gerald. I tricked him and had to go on the run."

He was shaking his head. "No, you can't convince me you're some kind of criminal. You're a good woman, Joanna. I don't know many women—or men—who'd do what you did for your friend Donovan. You're a mite reckless, I'd say; headstrong, like Travis."

A bitter laugh escaped her. "I'm reckless, all right. Reckless enough to think things would come out right if I could just find the courage to tell Travis who I was. I never figured on being accused of Cassie's crimes as well!"

"I think we can get to the bottom of that."

"What was all that about an annuity—fifty-thousand dollars? I thought Arne didn't have any money? Travis himself told me . . ."

"Brad and Sarah set up a special kind of insurance policy for Arne; it was supposed to give him a small income— enough to help him get along. They didn't just leave him some cash, because he had a habit of giving away whatever he had to anyone he thought needed it more. Trav used to get awful mad with him about that."

"Somehow that doesn't surprise me," Joanna said wryly.

"Well, anyway, the annuity was supposed to expire when Arne died—unless he had children."

"So that's why Travis—and Maggie, too—asked me if I was pregnant." Absently she raised her teacup to her lips. She almost scalded her mouth as she swallowed the hot liquid too quickly. "Barney, those bills! Cassie *did* have a baby!"

Barney nodded. "Looks that way. And a child with Arne's name gets the money in a lump sum—that's the way the policy reads. When Trav saw the dates on those bills, he knew you couldn't have been in two places at once. But he made the wrong connection. He thinks you're the real Cassie, and the other one is part of a trick to claim the money."

"Yes, I guess I can see how he could think that if he didn't stop to reason it out. I suppose I didn't help when I said Yes, I'd deceived him: we were talking about two different things!"

"Looks like you both jumped too quick. Joanna, all you have to do is tell him who you are; he'll understand, and you can make things right between you. I was sure glad when I saw you two were getting together. The difference you've made since you came, turning this lonesome place into a home again . . ."

Joanna jumped up and went to the screen door. She

looked out, barely aware of the soft breeze that carried the scent of pine and geraniums. Her head was beginning to ache; she felt the chill of old fears returning.

"No, Barney. He told me to leave, and that's what I'd better do. He'll clear things up with the real Cassie, but it's too late for anything else. I couldn't bear . . ." She broke off, her throat tightening up as she remembered the rejection on Travis' hard face. She would remember that until the day she died.

"But you've got to make it up with him, Joanna." Barney insisted, dismayed. "You owe him that much, don't you?"

"You think I didn't try? Travis doesn't listen very well."

"He was mad, that's all. Give him a chance. Where's he gone to, anyway?"

"Somewhere to register a protest about that water dispute. He went with John Temple."

"That means he went to the Capitol. No chance he'll get back before tomorrow. You'll have to wait here till he gets back."

"What for? Just so he can call me names again? I'm so tired of being on the wrong end of things."

"You love him, honey, and he loves you. That's why you've got to stick around and see this through. He'll understand. He's not in the clear on this himself, if you come to think about it. After all, if he'd taken time to make sure who you were in the bus station, the rest of it wouldn't have happened. Then he treated you so rough on account of Arne, it's no wonder you didn't feel like making explanations. Now he's gone off in a temper, but it won't last. He'll start to thinking, just like I did. We've all got our faults, and Travis' is being too damn hasty and hotheaded at times."

"Ha!" she laughed shortly, then fell silent, remembering how quick Travis had been to square off against Gerald in her defense at the party and in the park. How she had loved him for it—she had been glad for his hotheadedness then, hadn't she? But could she wait for him to cool down and then risk his rejecting her all over again? Some gambles came with stakes that were too high.

Blindly she raised her hand and pressed it against the screen, feeling the wire mesh between her fingers and the fresh air outside. Such a slight barrier, yet it was the difference between enclosure and freedom. God, she prayed, will I ever be on the other side, free of this fear? Shall I take the risk one more time?

"Okay, Barney," she heard herself saying. "I'll stick my neck out and wait until he gets back. If he's cooled down enough to listen, well, I'll tell him straight. If he doesn't like it, then I'll know it just wasn't to be. I'll pack my bag and go." She smiled tightly, her eyes bleak. "Maybe I'll go back to Denver and help Donovan fight Gerald. I've got a lot of aggravation built up in me that needs an outlet."

"That's the spirit, Joanna. You stick up for yourself and put it right. We'll see happy times here on the ranch before you know it!"

"I hope so. Things could hardly be more messed up than they are now."

But she was wrong. The next morning a strange car pulled up in front of the ranch house and the situation got very messy indeed.

Chapter Ten

Joanna was alone in the house, wondering for the hundredth time why she had agreed to wait until Travis returned. Barney had left early to take care of the chores, and, unable to settle down, she was in the living room thumbing through a magazine. The sound of a car door slamming made her jump. Was someone dropping Travis off? Her heart speeded up, and she hurried to the front window.

Walking toward the house was a thin young woman wearing a yellow jacket with oversize sleeves, knee-length culottes, and a pair of high-heeled boots. As she came up the steps she glanced toward the window and her sharp features took on a shuttered expression. Joanna hurried to the door, feeling an odd premonition.

"Is this the Carlyle place?" The woman's voice was husky but determined. Her eyes were a light indeterminate color, and she bore marks of experience on her youthful face. She couldn't have been more than twenty.

"Yes, it is." The premonition grew, and Joanna guessed what the young woman was going to say before she said it.

"I'm Cassie Carlyle."

Joanna gripped the door handle tightly. "Cassie . . . of course . . ." she said slowly, and the stranger looked at her oddly.

"I came to see Travis Carlyle. Is he in?"

Joanna shook her head to clear it. "Not just now. He's away from the ranch today."

"Well, how about asking us to come in? I've got a right, you know; I was married to his brother."

"Oh, yes, of course." Joanna pulled herself together and opened the door wider. "Come in." She stood aside, but the girl turned and beckoned, and Joanna realized Cassie was not alone. A husky youth of medium height climbed out of the car. He moved awkwardly because he was carrying a blanket-wrapped bundle from which emerged a thin wail. As the youth reached back inside for a large plastic bag, the cries gathered in strength and fury.

"Dammit, Joey, you've woken her up!" exclaimed Cassie. "Don't drop her, for heaven's sake!"

Since Cassie made no move to go to his assistance, Joanna stepped past her and hurried down the walk. Joey relinquished the baby into her arms with more haste than care, then turned back to get the bag. Joanna was glad to see a baby bottle protruding from one of the voluminous pockets and a box of diapers from another; it was obvious one of them was needed right away.

"Come on inside," she told the two young people, walking in ahead of them. She had to raise her voice to be heard. "I think we'd better do something for the baby."

"She's just hungry," Cassie said casually. "She doesn't like the bottle much, but that's all she gets. I haven't got any milk."

"No milk? We have plenty—oh, you mean . . ."

"I can't nurse her. But there's some formula in a thermos. All it needs is heating up."

They entered the family room. Joey put the diaper bag on the table and shoved both hands in his pockets. He looked uneasy yet defiant as he kept a wary eye on Joanna. Cassie sat down in the rocker, clearly unimpressed by the country kitchen.

She didn't seem to have much interest in the baby, either, Joanna thought while trying to shush its cries. "If one of you will take the baby, I'll warm up the bottle," she suggested. The tiny creature in her arms was getting tired; little hiccups punctuated the wailing cries.

With a sigh of exasperation, Cassie got up from the rocker and came to take the baby. "Okay. She probably needs changing, too."

As Joanna took out a pan and put water on to heat, she noticed that for all her offhanded attitude, Cassie was very careful. She changed the diaper efficiently and returned to the rocker with the baby cradled in her arms. When the bottle was warm, she held it to the tiny mouth, her sharp face softening as she looked down at her baby. Soon, only soft smacking noises broke the silence that fell in the room.

"Can I get you some coffee or fix you something to eat?" Joanna roused herself to make the offer. "You must be hungry. It's a long drive up here."

"It better not be for nothing," Joey muttered. He exchanged a glance with Cassie that caused her to thrust out her lip angrily.

"When will Travis get back?" Cassie demanded.

"I'm not sure, but Barney Olaffson, his partner, will be in soon."

"The old guy. Yeah, Arne told me about him. But it's Travis we need to see." Cassie's assurance faltered for a moment, and her bright lipstick seemed suddenly too strong a color for her pale complexion. "Well, we'll just have to wait, won't we? But I hope it's not too long, because we can't pay any extra fees on the car we rented to come here. Who are you, by the way? Arne said Travis wasn't married. You a live-in friend?"

"I'm Joanna Randall. I'm the housekeeper here, tempo-rarily." And that was about it, she thought with humor that bordered on the hysterical. Travis had the real Cassie now, though he didn't know it; she wondered if he would appreciate the bonus he was getting in the baby and Joey.

"Well, I got to hand it to you, sticking it out here in the boonies. Arne tried to get me to come out here, said he wanted Travis to meet me himself, not just hear about me secondhand. But I told him, no way! I like plenty of pavement around me. Arne had me fixed up with a place to stay in the city, and the doctor and all, so why should I come out to this godforsaken place?" The light eyes fixed on Joanna's, and she went on in nervous spurts, as though she'd rehearsed the words.

"I didn't know he was going to die so sudden, did I? I was pretty rocked by that telegram. All it said was ARNE DEAD. FUNERAL SATURDAY. ADVISE IF COMING. I was going to come, I even sent a telegram, but then the baby came early and I had all that trouble. I was pretty sick for a while; didn't care much about anything. Arne sure wasn't going to be able to help me anymore, was he?"

Joey moved uncomfortably. "Cassie . . ." he cautioned.

"I thought Joey wasn't going to come back, and then he did, and then the hospital got nasty about the bills, so I told them to send them to Arne's brother . . . I wouldn't have had the baby if it wasn't for Arne, so . . ."

"Shut up, Cassie," Joey said. "I came back, didn't I? Didn't I say I'd take care of you?"

"With what? No job, no money, no place to live? You know we need what Arne said he'd leave for the baby . . ."

They were interrupted. Joanna recognized Sally Temple's voice a moment before the kitchen door opened and the girl entered, followed by a dour-faced Travis.

"I don't see why you won't—" Sally stopped abruptly, her jaw dropping as she saw Joanna and the strangers in the kitchen.

Travis gently but firmly moved her out of the way and came inside. His glance was charged with a sudden flaring emotion when it fell on Joanna; then it swept over the newcomers. His eyes narrowed and his brows snapped into a forbidding dark line.

Joey had risen to face him. He looked nervous and pugnacious at the same time, his cheeks a little pale and his shoulders tensed.

"Are you Travis Carlyle?" he inquired, his voice higher than it had been.

"I'm Travis Carlyle. And you?"

Joanna held her breath.

"I'm Joey—I mean, I'm Joe Barnes, and this is my fiancée, Cassie." Joey waited a moment for a reaction. When Travis continued to stare at him, he went on nervously. "Cassie Carlyle. She married your brother, Arne."

Travis looked at Joanna. She felt hot and cold at the same time and could only look back at him, twisting her fingers into knots. The others were quiet, sensing something strained and unnatural in the way Travis and Joanna were staring at each other.

"My God," Travis said, exhaling. And then he asked the question he should have asked four weeks before. "Who are you?"

"Joanna Randall." She lifted her head proudly.

"Joanna . . . Randall."

Looking away from his stunned face, Joanna tossed a strained smile at Cassie. "Sorry—I borrowed your name for a while, Cassie. But you can have it back now."

Cassie's eyes narrowed suspiciously. "What do you mean, you borrowed my name? Is this some kind of trick to keep me from getting the money Arne promised me?" She rose from the rocker and came up to Travis, glaring aggressively at him. She turned toward Sally. "Here, kid, hold the baby. I want to get to the bottom of this."

Sally's arms went around the bundle of blankets and, after a look from Travis, she closed her mouth and sat down in the vacated rocker. She rocked agitatedly, mesmerized by the drama taking place before her eyes.

"Would somebody kindly make it clear"—Travis' voice made them jump—"just what the hell is going on?"

Unfortunately his voice also woke the baby, who immediately voiced her outrage. To Barney, coming in for lunch, it must have sounded like a creature in dire trouble, for he hurried in and looked around wildly.

"Trav, what's going on?" he cried anxiously.

Cassie raised her voice: "You must be Barney. Arne said you were the reasonable one. Would you tell Travis that I've come to collect on the promise Arne made to me, and he'd better not try to cheat me out of it."

It took him only a second, and Joanna had to admire Barney for his quick grasp of the situation. "You must be the real Cassie, then," he said. "And the baby, too. Glad to see you."

"Barney!" Travis roared. The baby stepped up the volume, and he flushed guiltily as everyone looked accusingly at him. "Barney," he repeated, "you know what's going on around here? Cassie just told me she wasn't . . ." he broke off, his brows reforming into a scowl as he ordered: "Do something about that noise!"

Joanna felt like making some noise herself. She wanted to laugh and cry at the same time. Where were her hopes for a calm, reasonable atmosphere where she could explain everything at last? Travis calm, cool, understanding?

Glaring at him, she said, "Let me have the baby." She took the squalling bundle from Sally. "The poor creature's been passed around so much, and everybody's made so much noise, no wonder she's upset. I'll take her into my room and you all can talk. What's her name, by the way?"

Cassie looked relieved. "Her name's Arnetta. Better take the diaper bag with you. When she gets mad, she wets a lot."

Travis made an abrupt gesture with his hand as though to prevent Joanna's quitting the scene, but she ignored him, only flashing him one sizzling look before she left the room.

The baby quiet at last, tucked between two pillows on her

bed, her lashes tiny half-moons on her damp cheeks, Joanna listened for sounds of battle from the other wing. It was just as well she had left the scene. She felt a simmering sensation somewhere inside that was threatening to erupt. Anger, disappointment, and frustration made a bad mix. And she *was* disappointed beneath the anger. In spite of knowing better, she had hoped he would immediately rush to her side, beg her forgiveness for leaving her like that.

A tap on the door called her back from her thoughts. The door opened and Travis came in. She put her finger to her lips and came over to him by the door.

"Joanna?" He seemed uncertain as he used her name for the first time. "I want to talk to you. I . . ."

"Shh," she whispered. "You'll wake the baby. Did you get everything straightened out?"

"Barney is fixing them something to eat. I think I got most of it, but I can't quite take it in. Look, why didn't you tell me . . . ?"

Sally called down the hall, "Travis, shall I unhitch the horses and put them in the corral?"

Joanna pushed Travis out into the hall and followed him, pulling the door closed behind her. "Hush! It took a long time to get Arnetta quiet, and I won't have you waking her up now!" Joanna glared at them both and Travis scowled.

"We've got to talk, dammit!"

"So we'll talk later—and don't swear at me!"

Expelling a deep breath of frustration, Travis turned on his heel and strode down the hall. Sally had already disappeared.

But they didn't get to talk; not privately. Joanna avoided it. She felt it would be a mistake to even try, with a houseful of people who kept popping up at inopportune moments. Besides, now that the truth was finally out, she was just getting used to being Joanna again. She was feeling less and less inclined to be apologetic about her perfectly understandable actions. If Travis wanted to start over on an equal footing this time, she'd be willing to listen. But he'd have to learn he was dealing with a different woman now, not the soft, submissive "Cassie" he had been used to.

She was alone with him briefly in the kitchen while she washed up the lunch dishes. He immediately seized the opportunity.

"Cassie—" Her freezing glance stopped him, then he started over in a low, urgent voice. "I mean, Joanna, dammit. Come out to the barn where we can talk. You've got to tell me . . ."

"Oh? What do I *have* to tell you?"

"You've got to explain why . . ."

She cut him off. "Do I really? I tried to explain before, and you wouldn't listen. You just rode off!" A lump filled her throat at the painful memory and she hardened her heart toward him.

"That was because—"

"Because you're a pigheaded, stubborn—"

"Confound it, how do you think I felt when I thought you were trying to pull off a con job?"

"Exactly! Just why did you jump to that conclusion? Barney didn't, and he didn't have any more to go on than you did!" She turned back to the sinkful of dishes, her cheeks flushing angrily. She grabbed a dish towel and thrust it at him. "Make yourself useful, can't you?"

He took the towel and began to dry the dishes. "You know when I asked you point-blank if you admitted to planning the whole thing from the first, you said yes. What was I supposed to think from that?"

"I only meant that when you picked me up at the station, I planned to let you go on thinking I was Cassie for a little while, that's all."

"I know that *now*, but how do you think it sounded then?"

"You could have given me the chance to explain!"

"I'm sorry about that. Cassie, I—"

"How many times do I have to tell you! My name is Joanna!"

He slammed a plate down on the counter and it broke neatly into two pieces. "How am I supposed to remember? I've been calling you Cassie for the last month—you didn't object then!"

They both reached for the broken plate and their hands touched. He grabbed and held her hand in his. She could see the frustration in his eyes as his grip tightened, pulling her closer. A twinge of guilt slipped through the guard she had put up against him, against the fear of his turning on her once more. She wasn't being fair to him; she was throwing away the chance to . . . "Travis," she began, her face softening.

Joey burst in through the door, dust-covered and with a rip on the knee of his trousers. "Mr. Carlyle, your cows—in that pen by the barn—I guess the gate was open. The cows got out, and they won't go back in."

"Damnation!" Travis roared, and Joanna jerked free from his hold.

"You're supposed to call them steers, Joey," she said, her softness vanished. "Travis likes to get the names right around here!"

Travis gave her a fulminating glance and then stalked out, closely followed by Joey, who was clearly excited by his first taste of cowboy life.

Later that evening, with Arnetta quiet in a blanket-lined drawer, they gathered in the living room for a conference. Barney sat near the baby, leaving the couch for Cassie and Joey. Travis leaned against the fireplace wall, his face showing lines Joanna had not seen before. He looked like he had slept as little as she had the night before.

"I'll say good night now," Joanna stated with a calm she wasn't feeling. Travis was making her terribly nervous with the way he watched her all the time. It was as though he were looking at her with new eyes and wasn't sure what to make of her yet. "You'll want to talk in private, and I have some packing to do," she finished, eager to escape.

"No!" Travis said sharply. Then he said in a more

normal tone, "I mean, would you please bring in some coffee or something? You might as well be in on this, too. I understand Cassie has already explained some of it to you."

His gaze was compelling, and a few minutes later she was aggravated to find herself making the coffee before she remembered that she hadn't planned to be at his beck and call anymore. Oh, well, as long as she was in the kitchen anyway. When she came back with the tray, she realized at once that Travis' questions had put the youngsters on the defensive.

"It was Arne's idea—the whole thing," Joey was saying hotly. "Sure, I took off; I didn't figure on being a father or anything like that. But I came back, and we're going to get married as soon as we—"

"As soon as you get the money from Arne's annuity?" Travis said dryly. "For your baby? The terms are that it be Arne's baby."

Flushed with anger, Joey fell silent. Cassie took up the cudgels in his defense. "Boy, you're sure not anything like Arne, are you? He knew the baby was Joey's; he said I didn't have to get an abortion—we'd get married and then he could do something for the baby, if it had his name. He said you probably wouldn't understand, since you didn't know me, but—"

"Arne was too softhearted for his own good."

"Arne was a great guy—the greatest! He never tried to take advantage, you know? He said the baby deserved a chance, and that if I didn't give it that chance, I'd hurt myself worse than the baby. He wouldn't quit until he got me to do it his way. Said the baby was his stake in the future—he knew he was going to die, didn't he?"

She wiped her hand across her eyes angrily. "I called the baby Arnetta, after him. He married me to make sure she got what he had to leave, so don't you go trying to take away what's rightfully hers! Joey—" Cassie turned her face into his shoulder and began to cry.

Travis telegraphed a look of appeal to Joanna, who went

to the young woman and took her hand. "Come on, now, Cassie," she chided softly. "You'll wake the baby. Don't worry about things anymore tonight. You've had a long journey today and you're tired. I've fixed up the spare bedroom, and you can have Arnetta in there with you. Why don't you go to bed now? Don't worry. Travis will do what's fair and right, you can be sure of that. You can trust him."

Joanna could feel Travis' eyes boring into her. She had spoken spontaneously, but she knew, even if she was still angry with him, that it was the truth. He would do what was right, for Cassie and for Arnetta.

Cassie stopped crying. She wiped her eyes with the back of her hand and said with an oddly dignified sniff, "That's all I ask. Just for what's fair and right."

Travis was looking at Joanna, his face enigmatic. "Joanna's right. It is late. Let's all get a good night's sleep and we'll talk about it tomorrow." He walked over to the corner and picked up the baby, drawer and all. He looked down into the sleeping face, and Joanna saw a shadow pass over his own dark features. "Come on, Arnetta Carlyle, it's time you were settled for the night."

Once in the bedroom wing, Cassie and Joey took over the settling of Arnetta, and Joanna turned toward her own room, aware that Travis was right behind her.

"Come back to the living room with me," he urged in a low voice. His eyes were turbulent with feelings that both excited and frightened her; the touch of his hand on her arm made her tremble.

The fear was followed by a flash of resentment. She had been on such a roller coaster of emotion with this man. What made him think she was willing to go along for another ride? Did he think all he had to do was grab her, and she'd fall to pieces for him?

"Not now, Travis, I'm too tired."

"We've got to straighten things out."

"You're probably right. But in the morning, after we've

both had some rest. Unless you don't want me sleeping here overnight? You did tell me to leave.''

''I didn't mean it!'' The accusing look in her eyes made him start over. ''That is, I meant it at the time, but . . .''

''Good night, Travis,'' she said firmly. She closed the door with him on the other side. An hour later the house was silent, but Joanna couldn't fall asleep.

Had she done the right thing? He seemed to want to talk to her badly enough, and in spite of his anger and frustration she was almost certain he wanted to take up where they had left off. But no, not this time. When they talked again, she didn't want any distractions, like his potent lovemaking, to get in the way of rational thinking. She couldn't trust her response to him. So their talk would have to take place when she was more sure of her control—both of her body and her temper, which right now was nearing the explosion point.

Her whole being seemed to be in revolt, triggered by the resumption of her own identity. She was Joanna Randall again, a woman independent of spirit, free of entanglements.

At least, she had been free of entanglements. She wasn't at all sure she wouldn't be better off becoming so again. But if she loved him? Groaning, she willed herself to calm down, and gradually she dropped off into uneasy sleep.

Much later she turned over, half-waking, and felt the bed give way on one side as a heavy body sat down. Her eyes flew wide, and she sat up in alarm, gasping.

''Shh . . . It's me, Travis,'' came the husky whisper.

''Travis! What are you doing here?'' she hissed, fright shaking her frayed nerves. By the moonlight that streamed into the room, she could see he was wearing a robe and very little else, if the wide expanse of his naked chest was any indication. The clean manly scent of his body reached her senses and she tensed to resist his appeal.

Travis chuckled ruefully. ''I'm trying to get the chance to talk to you, of course. I was in bed thinking, and as far as I can see, today will be as bad as last night. If we're going to talk privately, it's got to be now.''

"Well, I don't agree. I'm mad at you, Travis, and I'm likely to say something I'll regret if you don't let me cool down for a while.''

"You're mad at *me?* You're the one who said she trusted me, and then didn't tell me a little detail like her name was Joanna instead of Cassie. Why didn't you explain, Joanna? Barney told me about Denver, and Lasker, and your friend Donovan. Do you have any idea how I felt, hearing it from him instead of you?''

The pang of guilt she felt made her angrier. "I was going to explain everything Monday night, only you didn't come home, remember?''

"Sure I remember. I was at that meeting, trying to talk about water rights and federal legislation, when all I could think of was you.'' His hand had begun to stroke her arm where it lay outside of the sheets. Now it moved over the delicate structure of her collarbone, then lower to the lace at the neckline of her nightgown.

"Don't be angry.'' His voice was roughly enticing. His fingers slipped under the lace and his next words came out in a husky murmur: "We can settle it right now, right here . . .'' She gasped, almost forgetting the reason for being angry with him as his hand gently fondled her breast. Her traitorous flesh swelled and firmed and he groaned, "Sweetheart, you won't deny me? I need you so desperately! Cassie, my—''

"Joanna!'' she exclaimed indignantly. "My name is Joanna!''

"Joanna, Cassie . . .'' With a flick of his hand, he swept back the sheets, and his arms slid behind her, lifting her away from the pillow. "What does it matter what your name is? Kiss me, sweetheart; melt into my arms like you did before. Let me make love to you.''

He reached up to put her arms around his neck and then his parted lips were consuming hers; he followed her down to the pillow, his weight pressing urgently upon her. Her nightgown had ridden up her thighs, and there was nothing to hinder him from finding her naked vulnerability. The belt of his robe was loosened, and she knew for sure that he wore nothing beneath. He had come planning to seduce her! Like an idiot, she had made it easy for him, hadn't even locked the door.

Her simmering, uneven temper exploded. "You . . . you . . ." she sputtered furiously, yanking his head away from her mouth with fingers that gripped his hair painfully. "What do you mean it doesn't matter! It matters to me! Get off me, you big oaf!" Wriggling frantically beneath him, she struggled for leverage on the soft mattress.

Struck dumb with shock at her reaction, Travis moved to protect himself from her flailing limbs. He arched upward, his hand holding her thigh to hamper her movements.

"Calm down," he hissed. "All right, I won't do anything. Relax—I won't let you go till you calm down."

She lay still, her eyes blazing and huge; there was enough light to let him see that she was truly furious. Carefully he lifted himself away and released his hold on her thigh and shoulder. He sat up as she scrambled away from him and got out on the other side of the bed. She rushed to the light switch and flicked it on, then turned to impale him with blue eyes as cold as steel.

"I've had it, Travis Carlyle," she stated through set teeth. "I'm tired of trying to do everything your way; trying not to offend you, trying to win your approval. And all because I felt guilty for deceiving you. So okay, I shouldn't have done what I did! But it doesn't give you the right to come in here and treat me like a tramp!"

"I wasn't treating you like—"

"Oh, no? 'It doesn't matter what your name is, I just want to make love to you,'" she jeered in a parody of his words. "Well, I'm not just a warm body in a bed, here for your convenience!"

"That wasn't what I meant and you know it!"

Her breasts heaved. His eyes followed the movement, and she became aware that her thin nightgown was very little barrier to his hungry gaze. He had tightened the belt of his robe, but not before his image was emblazoned on her brain. She almost faltered, then resolutely she thrust the picture from her mind. She couldn't let her own desire undermine her determination to make a stand.

"There's only one thing I want from you right now, Travis, and that's your absence from this bedroom. I may have come here under false pretenses, looking for shelter, but I've worked damned hard for my keep. I'm entitled to one more night's sleep here. *Undisturbed* sleep,'' she underlined. She opened the door with a sweeping gesture, her nose and chin elevated disdainfully.

Her gesture, and Travis' thunderous brow as he stalked through the doorway, had an audience. Cassie and Joey were peering out of their half-opened door, wide-eyed. Travis stopped cold, uttered a brief but heartfelt phrase and stomped his way to his bedroom. He slammed the door behind him.

Two heads swiveled back to Joanna, and she looked heavenward, suppressing a colorful expression of her own. She shut her door gently, but the click of the lock reverberated down the hallway.

Chapter Eleven

In spite of a day outside that promised to be sunny and mild, Joanna faced the morning in a stormy mood. Her temper hadn't cooled in the short time before dawn had sent its first rays into her room. At last, after tossing and turning until her sheets and blanket were a tangled mess, she had gotten up and packed her suitcase. Enough was enough. She was getting out, as she should have done weeks ago. She dragged on her jeans and a top she hadn't gotten around to wearing so far, mostly because she had been uncertain of Travis' reaction. This morning it suited her mood perfectly. Short-sleeved, with a scoop neckline, the bright red fabric declared in neat white lettering, "This Ms. ain't mizzin' nothin'."

She prepared breakfast but left the food on the stove for everyone to help themselves. A skillet full of fried potatoes, chunks of beef, and onion made a savory hash. Scrambled eggs were piled on a heavy platter. Store bread was fine for toast, she decided, if anyone cared to fix it. She'd made her last biscuit in this house. She mixed a pitcher of orange juice from frozen concentrate and plunked it down on the table. Then she poured herself a cup of coffee and sat down.

Cassie came in, yawning. She looked at Joanna speculatively and helped herself to some scrambled eggs. Joey and Travis entered the room together. Travis' gray eyes studied Joanna at some length, as though he were assessing the exact state of her temper. He filled his plate without comment and sat down across from her at the table.

"Where's the baby?" asked Barney, hanging his hat on the peg next to Travis' by the door.

"In the bedroom, still sleeping," Cassie replied, blinking heavy eyes. "Don't worry, we'll be able to hear her when she wakes up."

Joanna looked at Travis and shared the fleeting gleam of amusement that appeared in his eyes. Hastily she looked back at her coffee cup.

"Aren't you going to have something besides coffee, Joanna? You didn't eat much last night, either."

"No, thanks, Barney. I've gained weight since I've been here; it's time I stopped eating such big meals." Immediately she regretted her hasty speech. Travis' interested stare at the upper part of her body told her he was calculating just where the extra weight had gone. A slight smile appeared on his face as he studied the message on her T-shirt; when he raised his eyes to her flushed face, the smile became mocking. Agitatedly she rose from the table and took her cup over to the sink.

Travis rose as well and brought his half-empty plate with him. Taking advantage of their partial isolation, he stood close to her and murmured in a low growl, "Look. We can't go on like this. Come out with me for a ride, and we can talk privately."

Joanna felt hemmed in. A memory flashed vividly across her mind of another time when he had held her against this same cabinet with the force of his anger, not the urgently persuasive expression that was on his face now.

"Me go riding with you?" she whispered back. "The

horse might run off with me, and you'd accuse me of horse theft. No, thanks.''

"You're not being fair—''

"Can I have a glass of water?'' Cassie spoke up. "I need to take some aspirin.''

"Of course,'' Joanna replied, relieved at the interruption. As she filled a glass she glanced quickly at Travis and saw his mounting frustration in the grim set of his mouth. The sight caused her to feel a certain satisfaction. It would be a while before she could forget that day.

Brushing past him, she went back to the table. The phone rang and Travis answered it. The rest of them listened unabashedly to the one-sided conversation.

"Yes,'' he said. "Yes, that was me.'' Pause. "I know all about that.'' Another pause. "He said to tell me what?'' A short laugh that was more of a bark ensued. "Okay, I'll tell her. And by the way, Donovan; I know it's Joanna. You don't have to call her Cassie anymore.''

Joanna was halfway out of her seat, but Travis had already hung up the phone. "Travis,'' she cried indignantly, "that call was for me. How dare you hang up!''

Travis looked smug as he strolled over to the door. "It wasn't for you. Your friend Donovan seems to have been in touch with your ex-boss in Denver. Lasker sent a message to you but sent it through me. I'm to tell you that, quote, your new man is too physical for his taste, and that as far as Lasker is concerned, he—meaning me—can have you. You're off the hook. Unquote. Donovan said the rest of it wasn't fit to quote. He also said to tell you not to worry; he's made a deal for the leases that puts him in clover. Said he and somebody named Kate are on their way to Reno for a wedding.''

Joanna was torn between gladness for Donovan and irritation at Travis' smugness. He had enjoyed passing that message along to her. Too physical indeed! He could have her, could he? Well, she'd see about that.

Travis took his Stetson from its peg and pulled it firmly down on his brow. In his hat, boots, low-slung jeans and open-necked shirt, he looked exactly like the hero of a western movie, except for the missing gunbelt, she thought scathingly, tearing her gaze away from him with an effort. Looking at the others, she saw that Joey's face was showing signs of wistful envy, and even Cassie looked impressed.

"I'll saddle up the horses, Joanna." Travis' gaze dropped again to the lettering on her T-shirt and his mouth widened in a sudden confident grin. "I'm looking forward to our ride. Don't disappoint me. Otherwise, I'll have to come get you."

"What about us?" Cassie asked aggrievedly. "You said we'd talk this morning."

His casual wave dismissed her grievance. "We can talk this afternoon. Look around, why don't you? Get acquainted with the animals, take a walk, climb a hill." Gray eyes glittered at Joanna as he named the things that had filled so many of her spare hours with pleasure and interest. Travis slanted his hat lower over his eyes and walked out, whistling.

A slow burn suffused Joanna. She knew what he was up to. He had made up his mind to take her off into the hills and seduce her, confound him! But she wasn't going to let him get away with it. If he wanted to make things right with her, he was going to have to deal with the woman she really was, not the woman he thought he knew. He'd rejected her once, devastatingly. She'd have to be shown pretty conclusively that he truly cared if she was ever to forget those terrible moments. But how could she be sure? Don't disappoint *him,* he'd said. He'd said . . .

The others looked at her in surprise as she leapt from her chair. Her eyes were bright with resolution as she said, "Joey, Cassie—can I take your rental car back for you? I'll pay the fees. Barney or Travis will take you into town when you're ready to go. You might be here for some time."

Cassie poked Joey with her elbow and he responded, "We got the car at that garage in town, after we got off the bus. I suppose . . ."

"Joanna, you can't go now, just when things are all getting settled," Barney said worriedly.

Joanna went over to him and hugged him hard. She kissed his cheek. "There's something I have to find out, Barney. If things don't work out, I want you to know you're the nicest thing that's happened to me in years. I won't forget how kind you've been to me."

He saw the determination in her face and his expression became resigned. "Okay, honey. You have to work things out your own way. You'll write and let us know how you are? You never know . . ."

"That's right—you never know," she smiled, blinking mistily. She turned back to Joey and knew it was the plea in her eyes as well as the opportunity to save the rental fees that made him hand the keys over to her. In five minutes, she was on her way down the road. Barney waved to her from the veranda, a dwindling figure in the rearview mirror.

Prospect looked about the same to Joanna. Still on the small side, still not bustling, but rather attractive with its cheerful shop windows on Main Street and the spot of green color in the public square where she and Travis and Gerald had acted out their brief drama. Between the library building and the spreading branches of a tree, she could see the mountain peaks that appeared so close. The fragmentary view was the same as the view from the window in Travis' room at the homestead.

For a little while there, I thought I was going to see the mountains in winter, she thought wistfully. It must be spectacularly beautiful here then. She thought of the honey-colored sheepskin jacket hanging in the closet back at the ranch, and a lump formed in her throat. We could have gone skiing together, she mused. Made snowmen. Sat before the fire and sipped hot chocolate while the winter storms beat against the old homestead's sturdy walls.

Preoccupied with her thoughts, she drove past the garage where Joey had hired the car, then had to go back. The rental fees were soon dealt with. She walked the couple of blocks over to the bus station, carrying her suitcase. It seemed much lighter without the manila envelope that had caused her so much trouble. The back street that housed the station seemed pleasant enough in the bright sunlight, but the station interior looked as bleak as she remembered. She sat down in the same hard chair by the window.

He's not coming, she acknowledged at last, stricken. There had been time and more, if he cared enough. It had been a foolhardy gamble, and she had lost. It was hard to remember just why she had done it. Had she really hoped he would understand and come after her—by choice and not by chance?

With wide aching eyes, she stared out through the window with the broken blind, not caring that the day was beautiful, the sun shining. Why didn't I talk to him when he wanted to? she agonized. Now I've lost him. He'll go back to someone like that Sue Ann at the party, some woman who will never love him as I do. She suppressed a sob. With the complication of Cassie and her baby to deal with, it was obviously a relief to him that she had taken this way out. No good-byes. It must have been embarrassing for him to come home and find her still there.

After delaying as long as she could bear to, Joanna went up to the ticket window. The clerk was not the same as the one she remembered. After a brief exchange about her ticket to Cheyenne and an observation on the weather, he left her to wait the hour before her bus was expected. She sat down on the familiar hard seat, her suitcase beside her, and closed her eyes to keep the scalding tears from sliding down her cheeks.

This time Joanna heard the screech of brakes outside the

terminal. When the door crashed open she was already looking, galvanized to see the tall figure standing in the opening, eyes blazing from under the brim of his Stetson. Grease marred Travis' shirt and arms, and grim determination pulled his mouth into a hard line. With predatory intent, he came toward her and halted, dangerously close. His hands fastened onto her arms and lifted her effortlessly out of her seat to stand on her suddenly boneless legs.

Her heart was ringing bells and clanging cymbals: he had come after all! Through wet tangled lashes she stared up at him, unable to speak. She didn't even feel the painful tightening of his hands on her arms.

"Joanna . . ." He swallowed hard, then bit off his next words as the clerk appeared in the ticket window, drawn by the noise.

"Howdy, Trav," the clerk began, his eyes bright with curiosity.

" 'Day, Chet." Travis' clipped tone discouraged further comment. He let go of Joanna with one hand and grabbed the suitcase. Keeping a firm grip on her arm, he urged her toward the door.

"What . . . ?" Outside Joanna dug in her heels after almost tripping in the effort to keep up with his giant strides. "Travis! Where do you think you're going?"

His look blended exasperation and pleading in equal amounts. "Get in the truck, Joanna—please!" She was practically lifted into the cab. He slammed the door, shutting off her protest at his high-handedness.

They followed the now familiar route back toward the ranch. "I've got a bus to catch in less than an hour, Travis," she said, not quite daring to believe her gamble had paid off.

His comment was succinct, colorful, and amounted to "Over my dead body."

"I told you not to swear at me," she said severely.

"Look," he said after a quick glance at her. His wary expression told her he was not at all sure of her reaction to his practically kidnapping her. "We've got to talk! We'd be interrupted in town, at the ranch, and probably on the moon if we were there. I know a place along the canyon where I can guarantee all the privacy we need."

"For what?" she asked suspiciously.

Another glance, then he said carefully, "For a long overdue conversation between one Ms. Joanna Randall and Mr. Travis Cochise Carlyle. I believe they need to get acquainted. *Before* any other . . . er, interesting activities take place."

"Cochise?" she asked, diverted, though a tiny corner of her heart was palpitating madly at the suggestion of those future interesting activities.

"Cochise," he repeated with a downward grin at her. His diversion had been deliberate, she knew. "My mother's mother came from a related tribe. It was thought I might have inherited some of the genes." He smiled his wolfish smile, and after her heart slowed again, she had to agree inwardly that his grandmother had been right.

They reached a wide bend in the canyon road and pulled off. An overgrown rutted road straggled off at an angle, and Travis drove the truck up the track until they were out of sight of the main road. A rock slide ahead, an old one from the look of the shrubs and plants growing up between the fallen boulders, blocked the track and made it unusable. The truck stopped. Travis pulled the brake on forcibly and turned to her.

Out of the many thoughts careening wildly around in her head, Joanna pulled one and blurted out before he could speak: "Why were you so long in coming after me?"

"Would you believe that repair job we did on the carburetor didn't hold up? I was right behind you when the motor quit. Why the hell did you take off like that?" His eyes glittered, but she saw the hurt that lay behind his roughly spoken words. His hand was clenched tightly as it rested on the steering wheel.

"I'm not sure . . . I thought I needed to find out if you

cared enough to come after me. I couldn't be sure. After the other day . . .''

His hand unclenched and came up to touch her mouth, then dropped to her shoulder, curving around it almost hesitantly. Pain showed in his eyes and he spoke with difficulty: ''I couldn't have borne it if you had left me, Joanna. With all the rest of the confusion and mix-up, I knew that. I can't believe I actually told you to leave. All the time I was away, I kept hearing myself telling you to be gone when I got back, and I almost went out of my mind. When I made it home at last and saw you hadn't left, I could have dropped with relief. Then, last night—''

''Yes, about last night!'' Remembered indignation sparked in her eyes. ''Do you realize what it sounded like when you said it didn't matter what my name was, you just wanted me?''

''I didn't mean it the way it sounded, honey.''

''Joanna!'' Her eyes flashed.

''Joanna, honey, Cassie—they're just names that mean *you!* Nobody else. It's you, you aggravating, tormenting, deceiving witch!'' Travis' eyes sparked with temper also. ''After calling you Cassie for a month, it's not surprising that the name slips out once in a while. But it's *you* I want to hold in my arms like this . . .'' He yanked her against his chest. ''Kiss like this . . .'' His mouth enveloped hers. After a long, long moment, he raised his head only to murmur throatily, ''Make love to you like this . . .''

He possessed her quivering lips once more. Emotions held firmly in check for too long were suddenly unleashed in an explosion of mutual need. With passionate fire they kissed, and the world vanished around Joanna as the sensual movement of his lips on hers robbed her of all sense but the knowledge that this was where she belonged. She gave herself up to him wholly. Flames began to dance inside her, and her fingers tightened in his hair. His breathing, rapid and no longer silent, told her the flames were alight in him as well. She felt the tremor that shook him when, after a timeless period that began to ease the aching hurts deep inside her, he reined in the desires that would have robbed them both of self-control.

He pressed his face into the curve of her neck and shoulder and spoke hoarsely, his voice taut with emotion: "Oh, love, last night . . . it wasn't just anybody I needed and wanted. It was only you. . . . I love you."

Unable to speak, Joanna stroked his cheek with a trembling hand, the movement speaking for her. He held her in a gentling embrace, and in a little while they became calmer as the flames inside them gradually subsided.

"Promise me you won't run away from me again, sweetheart? I know I hurt you, behaved badly by not believing in you like Barney did. I haven't made you afraid of me, have I?"

"Not of you, darling. Of my own feelings. It's not easy for me to talk about it, but really trusting in someone besides myself scares me silly. There's so much risk of being hurt."

"I know. It cuts both ways, honey."

"Yes." Tentatively, she raised her hand and caressed his cheek. He had forgotten to shave that morning, and there was a dark haze along his jaw and cheek line.

"Joanna . . ." he said softly, tasting the name on his tongue. "Kind of old-fashioned, but strong. Yes, it sounds like you. Loving and good; loyal to your friends and generous with your compassion. A woman for a man to love and cherish all his days."

He looked searchingly into her eyes. "Can you live here in the mountains with me, Joanna? I thought I'd never leave this place, but if you couldn't be happy here, I'd be willing to try living in your world."

He meant it. Joanna felt a constriction in her throat; he couldn't have made it more clear that what he felt for her was far stronger than the early youthful love he had given to Christine. For her, he hadn't been prepared to give up his heritage. For Joanna, he was willing to do whatever was necessary for them to be together. Old fears receded, became dim, and her voice shook with emotion as she spoke the words that opened the door into a world she had thought she would never enter.

"I fell in love with you here, Travis. I've lived in so many places that 'home' hasn't had much meaning to me. If you love me . . .''

Travis took her hand and raised it to his lips.

"If you love me," she went on, "then where you are is home to me." She turned her fingers in his hand to touch his lips, and the responsive movement under her fingertips filled her with a warm wave of delight. "But I'm not making any great sacrifice. I fell in love with the mountains, too, and with your family, and your home. They're part of you, and I've felt very lonely at the thought that I would never be a part of it with you.''

"Darling . . .'' The emotion in his voice thrilled her as he tenderly took her in his arms again. "Darling Joanna . . .''

"After all,'' she continued before he could begin kissing her again. Her smile widened and her eyes glowed. "I don't think we could get Ezekiel Carlyle's four-poster in any apartment in the city—and where would we put Barney? No, I think we'd better stay here. Though you haven't exactly made it clear just what my status is supposed to be. I got the impression at the party that my living with you alone at the ranch is regarded as highly questionable. I don't mind, but—''

His growl halted her. "There'll be no question about it. We'll get married and that will settle the clacking tongues.''

"If you think a wedding is going to stop the talk, you're dreaming!'' Joanna declared with a gurgle of amusement. "What do you think Sally is doing right now? Broadcasting the interesting news that there are two 'Cassies' at the Carlyle household, along with a baby that might or might not be Arne's, and one or two other fascinating facts, that's what! We've given the community enough material for ten years worth of gossip!'' She regarded him closely and a little anxiously, since she had been responsible for most of it.

Travis grinned wryly. ''I'd forgotten about that. Well, we'll just have to tough it out. We can take off on our honeymoon and trust Barney and Maggie to handle it. With any luck the worst of it will be over by the time we get back, and we'll live down the rest in time.''

''Travis, tell me straight. Can you forget the way we met, the fact that I deceived you, all the rest? I can't live the rest of my life under a cloud of guilt. If you threw it up to me every time we had an argument, I wouldn't be able to take it.''

''Honey, I can't forget the way I treated *you*. If I hadn't been so wrapped up in my own pride and resentment for the way I thought Arne had been treated, I would have investigated and been able to help Cassie the way Arne wanted her to be helped.'' His arms around her tightened, as though for comfort. ''I've tried to understand why he didn't confide in me, and I know it was my fault. He couldn't trust me not to fly off the handle about it, spoil his plan. I think he intended to tell me, there at the last, but he left it until too late. So if anyone should have guilt feelings, it's me, not you.''

Joanna saw the regret that shadowed his eyes and hugged him in sympathy. ''You can make up for it, Travis. Cassie still needs your help.''

He nodded. ''I already asked Barney to call the lawyer and get things started on the transfer. Little Arnetta will have her chance, just the way Arne wanted.''

''That's all any of us need, isn't it? Just a chance. To grow up in a reasonable environment, to meet someone we love, to be happy. . . .''

His finger stroked her cheek, raised her chin so he could look in her eyes. ''I owe Arne for my chance, too. I'll never regret coming to find 'Cassie' that night in the bus station. Taking you home was the best thing I ever did.''

"I know." Joanna smiled at him mischievously. "Though I had my doubts when I bumped into that stuffed creature in the hall that first night."

"That elkhead is an heirloom, I'll have you know. Ezekiel shot it one hard winter before the ranch got started. I probably wouldn't be here today if it weren't for that elk."

"Well, heirloom or no heirloom, I don't like the way it sneers at me sometimes. No, honestly," she laughed as he looked at her with a disbelieving grin. "It keeps telling me I'm just a tenderfoot from the city who doesn't know beans about how to get along in the wilds, and—"

His arms tightened around her once more. "In that case, we'll get rid of it. Nothing and no one is going to chase you away from me."

"No?" she murmured, distracted by the fascinating lights that danced in the depths of the gray eyes looking into hers.

"No. Barney admires that head. We'll let him keep it in his cabin, and let our descendants decide its ultimate fate."

"Descendants? You mean there're going to be more of you Carlyles for me to handle?"

"Mmm-hmm . . . If you want . . . ?" A question edged his words.

A curious yearning stirred deep within her. "Yes . . ." she said huskily, "yes, I want that too." His head was coming nearer. Her eyes focused on his mouth, and her own lips parted in anticipation. "I think we should get started on those descendants soon—very soon." With a sigh, Joanna settled into the haven of his arms—home at last.

EYE OF THE STORM

MAURA SEGER

A powerful
portrayal of
the events of
World War II in the
Pacific, *Eye of the Storm* is a riveting story of how love
triumphs over hatred. In this, the first of a three-book
chronicle, Army nurse Maggie Lawrence meets Marine
Sgt. Anthony Gargano. Despite military regulations
against fraternization, they resolve to face together
whatever lies ahead.... Author Maura Seger, also known
to her fans as Laurel Winslow, Sara Jennings, Anne
MacNeil and Jenny Bates, was named 1984's
Most Versatile Romance Author by *The Romantic Times*.

At your favorite bookstore in March or send your name, address and zip or
postal code, along with a check or money order for $4.25 (includes 75¢ for
postage and handling) payable to Harlequin Reader Service to:

HARLEQUIN READER SERVICE

In the U.S.
Box 52040
Phoenix, AZ 85072-2040

In Canada
5170 Yonge Street
P.O. Box 2800
Postal Station A
Willowdale, Ont. M2N 6J3

EYE-C-1

Fall in love again for the first time every time you read a Silhouette Romance novel.

If you enjoyed this book, and you're ready to be carried away by more tender romance...get 4 romance novels FREE when you become a Silhouette Romance home subscriber.

Act now and we'll send you four touching Silhouette Romance novels. They're our gift to introduce you to our convenient home subscription service. Every month, we'll send you six new Silhouette Romance books. Look them over for 15 days. If you keep them, pay just $11.70 for all six. Or return them at no charge.

We'll mail your books to you two full months *before they are available anywhere else.* Plus, with every shipment, you'll receive the Silhouette Books Newsletter absolutely free. *And Silhouette Romance is delivered free.*

Mail the coupon today to get your four free books—and more romance than you ever bargained for.

Silhouette Romance is a service mark and a registered trademark.

------- MAIL COUPON TODAY -------

Silhouette Romance®
120 Brighton Road, P.O. Box 5084, Clifton, N.J. 07015-5084

☐ Yes, please send me FREE and without obligation, 4 exciting Silhouette Romance novels. Unless you hear from me after I receive my 4 FREE books, please send me 6 new books to preview each month. I understand that you will bill me just $1.95 each for a total of $11.70—with no additional shipping, handling or other charges. **There is no minimum number of books that I must buy, and I can cancel anytime I wish.** The first 4 books are mine to keep, even if I never take a single additional book.

☐ Mrs. ☐ Miss ☐ Ms. ☐ Mr.   BRR3L5

Name _____ (please print)

Address _____ Apt No _____

City _____ State _____ Zip _____
( )
Area Code   Telephone Number

Signature (If under 18, parent or guardian must sign.)

This offer, limited to one per customer, expires June 30, 1985. Terms and prices subject to change. Your enrollment is subject to acceptance by Silhouette Books.

SRR-R-A

Four exciting
First Love from Silhouette
romances yours for 15 days—*free!*

These are the books that girls everywhere are reading and talking about, the most popular teen novels being published today. They're about things that matter most to young women, with stories that mirror their innermost thoughts and feelings, and characters so real they seem like friends.

To show you how special First Love from Silhouette is, we'd like to send you or your daughter four exciting books to look over for 15 days—absolutely free—as an introduction to the First Love from Silhouette Book Club.℠ If you enjoy them as much as we believe you will, keep them and pay the invoice enclosed with your trial shipment. Or return them at no charge.

As a member of the Club, you will get First Love from Silhouette books regularly—delivered right to your home. Four new books every month for only $1.95 each. You'll always be among the first to get them, and you'll never miss a title. There are never any delivery charges and you're under no obligation to buy anything at any time. Plus, as a special bonus, you'll receive a *free* subscription to the First Love from Silhouette Book Club newsletter!

So don't wait. To receive your four books, fill out and mail the coupon below *today!*

First Love from Silhouette is a service mark and registered trademark.

First Love from Silhouette®

120 Brighton Road, P.O. Box 5084, Clifton, N.J. 07015-5084

YES, please rush me 4 First Love from Silhouette books to look over for 15 days absolutely *free*. Unless you hear from me after I receive them, send me 4 new First Love from Silhouette books each month, plus my free newsletter subscription. I understand that you will bill me only $7.80 for each shipment, with no additional shipping, handling or other hidden charges. **There is no minimum number of books that I must buy, and I can cancel anytime I wish.**

BFR3S5

Name	*(please print)*	
Address		Apt. #
City	State	Zip

Signature (If under 18, parent or guardian must sign)

This offer, limited to one per customer, expires June 30, 1985. Terms and prices subject to change. Your enrollment is subject to acceptance by Silhouette Books.

FL-OP-A

Let Silhouette Inspirations show you a world of Christian love and romance... for 15 days, free.

If you want to read wholesome love stories...with characters whose spiritual values are as meaningful as yours...then you'll want to read Silhouette Inspirations™ novels. You'll experience all of love's conflicts and pleasures—and the joy of happy endings—with people who share your beliefs and goals.

These books are written by Christian authors...Arlene James, Patti Beckman, Debbie Macomber, and more...for Christian readers. Each 192-page volume gives you tender romance with a message of hope and faith...and of course, a happy ending.

We think you'll be so delighted with Silhouette Inspirations, you won't want to miss a single one! We'd like to send you 2 books each month, as soon as they are published, through our Home Subscription Service. Look them over for 15 days, free. If you enjoy them as much as we think you will, pay the enclosed invoice. If not, simply return them and owe nothing.

A world of Christian love and spirituality is waiting for you...in the pages of Silhouette Inspirations novels. Return the coupon today!

Silhouette Inspirations Home Subscription Service
120 Brighton Road, P.O. Box 5084, Clifton, N.J. 07015-5084

Yes, I'd like to receive two new Silhouette Inspirations each month as soon as they are published. The books are mine to examine for 15 days, free. If I decide to keep the books, I will pay only $2.25 each, a total of $4.50. If not delighted, I can return them and owe nothing. There is never a charge for this convenient home delivery—no postage, handling, or any other hidden charges. *I understand there is no minimum number of books I must buy, and that I can cancel this arrangement at any time.*

☐ Mrs.   ☐ Miss   ☐ Ms.   ☐ Mr.   BCR3P5

Name	(please print)

Address		Apt. #

City	State	Zip
( )		

Area Code	Telephone Number

Signature (If under 18, parent or guardian must sign)

This offer, limited to one per customer, expires June 30, 1985. Terms and prices subject to change. Your enrollment is subject to acceptance by Silhouette Books.

SILHOUETTE INSPIRATIONS is a trademark and service mark.

I-OP-A

READERS' COMMENTS ON
SILHOUETTE ROMANCES:

"The best time of my day is when I put my children to bed at naptime and sit down to read a Silhouette Romance. Keep up the good work."

P.M.*, Allegan, MI

"I am very fond of the quality of your Silhouette Romances. They are so real. I have tried to read some of the other romances, but I always come back to Silhouette."

C.S., Mechanicsburg, PA

"I feel that Silhouette Books offer a wider choice and/or variety than any of the other romance books available."

R.R., Aberdeen, WA

"I have enjoyed reading Silhouette Romances for many years now. They are light and refreshing. You can always put yourself in the main characters' place, feeling alive and beautiful."

J.M.K., San Antonio, TX

"My boyfriend always teases me about Silhouette Books. He asks me, how's my love life and naturally I say terrific, but I tell him that there is always room for a little more romance from Silhouette."

F.N., Ontario, Canada

*names available on request